Rooted in Sin

A Dark Mafia Romance

Chicago Sin
Book 2

Alta Hensley

Renee Rose

Copyright © June 2023 Rooted in Sin by Alta Hensley, Renee Rose and Renee Rose Romance

All rights reserved. This copy is intended for the original purchaser of this book ONLY. No part of this book may be reproduced, scanned, or distributed in any printed or electronic form without prior written permission from the authors. Please do not participate in or encourage piracy of copyrighted materials in violation of the authors' rights. Purchase only authorized editions.

Published in the United States of America

Wilrose Dream Ventures LLC and Alta Hensley

Cover by: Pop Kitty Designs

This book is a work of fiction. While reference might be made to actual historical events or existing locations, the names, characters, places and incidents are either the product of the authors' imaginations or are used fictitiously, and any resemblance to actual persons, living or dead, business establishments, events, or locales is entirely coincidental.

This book contains descriptions of many BDSM and sexual practices, but this is a work of fiction and, as such, should not be used in any way as a guide. The author and publisher will not be responsible for any loss, harm, injury, or death resulting from use of the information contained within. In other words, don't try this at home, folks!

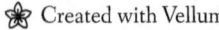 Created with Vellum

Contents

Want FREE Renee Rose books?	v
Chapter 1	1
Chapter 2	9
Chapter 3	15
Chapter 4	21
Chapter 5	27
Chapter 6	35
Chapter 7	45
Chapter 8	49
Chapter 9	55
Chapter 10	63
Chapter 11	67
Chapter 12	75
Chapter 13	81
Chapter 14	87
Chapter 15	93
Chapter 16	101
Chapter 17	107
Chapter 18	113
Chapter 19	121
Chapter 20	131
Chapter 21	139
Chapter 22	145
Chapter 23	151
Chapter 24	157
Chapter 25	163
Chapter 26	171
Chapter 27	177
Chapter 28	183
Chapter 29	187

Chapter 30	193
Chapter 31	201
Chapter 32	207
Epilogue	217
Also by Alta Hensley	221
Other Titles by Renee Rose	225
About Alta Hensley	231
About Renee Rose	233

Want FREE Renee Rose books?

Go to http://subscribepage.com/alphastemp to sign up for Renee Rose's newsletter and receive a free copy of *Alpha's Temptation, Theirs to Protect, Owned by the Marine* and more. In addition to the free stories, you will also get bonus epilogues, special pricing, exclusive previews and news of new releases.

Chapter One

Hannah

A car screeches into the alleyway behind Garden of Eden, my flower shop.

Armando's cousin, Marco, who was stationed in the alleyway to protect me, whirls, hand reaching for the gun strapped to his side.

I instinctively flinch, my heart stopping. A guy leans out of the open window, gun raised and aimed directly at us. Time seems to slow as Marco's eyes widen with realization. "Get down!" He lunges toward me, throwing me to the cold concrete ground behind the garbage dumpster.

Marco's body shields mine as the deafening sound of gunfire fills the alleyway. He lifts his gun to return fire, but before he can, he's hit.

Pain flares in his eyes. His body jerks.

I scream. Blood splatters everywhere, and some of it pools on my legs, hot and sticky.

"Marco!" My voice is barely audible over the cacophony of gunfire hitting the metal dumpster.

My hands tremble as I reach out to touch him, the

reality of the situation sinking in. This is no random act of violence—we were targeted.

"Stay down," he grits through clenched teeth, his body trembling from shock or adrenaline.

Even as his blood pools between us, he never takes his eyes off me, as if determined to protect me at all costs.

Oh God.

I've already seen one man die in the last week. Already been exposed to the violence of Armando's life. But that death felt surreal. Like watching a movie. Marco is a man I know. Armando's cousin. If he dies–

No, I can't even think it. He's still breathing. He seems alert.

Voices shout from the car, "That's not him" and "Go! Go! Go! Go!" It speeds away, leaving a cloud of dust and the sound of squealing tires as the only evidence of the drive-by.

That's not him.

They were trying to kill Armando, and they came to my shop. To the alleyway behind it. Does that mean they've connected me to him?

Is he no longer safe in my apartment?

That thought chokes me.

Marco's blood keeps draining, staining my clothes and skin. He groans and rolls partway off me, trying to push himself up.

"Take it easy. I'll call for help."

I search for my phone and see it cast to the side. *Armando.* I was speaking to Armando before this all happened.

"Armando!" I cry out, trying to pull my legs out from under Marco's. "Armando, Marco's hit!" Maybe he can still hear what's happening and now knows we are both alive but in danger.

Almost as if summoned by my voice, Armando appears at the mouth of the alleyway, his eyes wide with panic. He takes in the scene before him—Marco injured and me covered in blood and shaking uncontrollably.

"Hannah!" He runs to us, but his gaze is only on me.

"I'm okay, but Marco's hit."

"*Madonna mia*, what the fuck happened?" He crouches beside us, his hands hovering over Marco, like he's unsure where to touch or how to help. Fear is etched on his pale face, a vulnerability I've never seen from him before.

"Your buddies," Marco groans, shifting to sit up and gritting his teeth against the pain. "They came out of nowhere."

"Did you get a chance to see who they were?" Armando demands. I can see the gears turning in his head, already planning retaliation.

"I-I don't know," I stammer, still in shock. "I didn't see their faces."

"Fuck." Armando's gaze shifts between Marco and me, his concern palpable. "We need to get you both somewhere safe. Can you walk?"

"Of course I can walk," Marco scoffs, trying to climb to his feet. His face contorts with pain, and he collapses back onto the ground. Armando's jaw clenches, and he picks up Marco's arm to wrap around his shoulder, heaving him to his feet.

"Yeah, you're not walking anywhere like this."

I move to the other side of Marco to help. Together, we manage to hoist Marco to his feet, each of us taking one of his arms over our shoulders.

"Mando," Marco says quietly, his voice strained. "I didn't see it coming."

"We'll worry about that later," Armando clips. "Right now, we need to focus on getting you both out of here."

As we half-carry, half-drag Marco out of the alleyway toward my shop, my thoughts whirl with a gut-wrenching realization: my life has become irrevocably intertwined with this dangerous world and the man who brought me into it. Not that witnessing him kill a man with his bare hands hadn't already bound us together.

Blood soaks the back of Marco's leg, and I see Armando take it in, his nostrils flaring. "We need to get you to the hospital," he says.

"I'm fine," Marco insists through gritted teeth as I try to steady him on his feet. "Just get one of the guys to dig the bullet out."

"Shut up," Armando snaps. "I'm taking you to the hospital. Give me your keys." He props his cousin up against the brick wall by my back door.

"Dude, I don't want blood on the seats of the Beamer."

"You'd rather go in an ambulance?"

He makes a growling sound in his throat. "Fine." Marco reluctantly gives up his keys.

"Can you hold him up for a minute, Flowers? I'll pull the car around."

"Of course." My voice breaks. I'm still shaking all over, in total shock.

Armando must catch the fear in my voice because he pauses, gaze roaming over me again, as if he's still searching for any sign of injury.

"I'm okay," I promise. "Go get the car."

Worry clouds his dark eyes. "Are you sure?"

I nod, trying to ignore the lingering fear that clings to me like a second skin. "I'm fine. Really. Go!"

He gives a jerky nod and jogs away.

A few minutes later, a BMW zips into the alleyway and stops. Armando throws open the passenger door, then climbs out to help me get Marco into it. I climb into the back seat.

"You should just dump me in the front," Marco says when Armando takes off. "I wouldn't want this to affect your parole."

Armando's jaw tightens. "This is my fucking fault," he snaps.

"Quit your pity party, *stronzo*. I'm the one who got shot. You're gonna drop me in front and drive away. Call Leo and make sure he keeps it from our ma then come in with him when he arrives, like you just found out."

Armando looks grim, but nods. I see him checking the rear view mirror at me.

"I'll go in with him," I say. "I'm not on parole."

"No," Armando says immediately. "I don't want you tied to this in any way. *Capito?*"

At the hospital, Armando speeds up to the curb of the Emergency area. "Hey, *caging*," Marco rasps. "Don't worry about me. Just a flesh wound." He throws open his door and tumbles out, somehow managing to stagger toward the entry.

"I should go with him."

"Stay," Armando growls, his gaze on his cousin for a moment longer before he guns the car and peels out.

He circles the hospital then pulls into the parking area and shuts off the car. Armando's hands shake as he pulls out his phone. "I need to call Leo," he mutters, gaze darting around the parking lot as if expecting another attack at any moment.

"Leo, it's me." Armando's voice is thick with urgency when Marco's brother answers. "Marco's been shot.... In the alleyway at Garden of Eden. He was protecting Hannah. It was meant for me. Yeah, we're at Cook County now. Meet me here. And Marco said to keep this from your ma."

The conversation ends quickly, and Armando slips his phone back into his pocket.

When we get out of the car, he's still scanning me for injuries, like he thinks I secretly got shot and didn't tell him.

"Are you hurt?"

I shake my head.

"Let me see," he insists.

He wraps an arm around my waist, guiding me closer to him. His touch sends shivers down my spine, but it's exactly what I need to quiet the shaking in my limbs. It grounds me.

Armando's hands move gently over my body, checking for any injuries. He growls at the scrapes on my knees from the pavement. "Fuck, Hannah. Thank God you weren't hit." He drops his forehead against mine.

"Armando..." I begin, unsure of what to say or do.

"I'm sorry, Hannah." Armando's arm remains wrapped around me, his breathing ragged as he surveys our surroundings, his gaze darting from one shadowy corner to the next. I sense the tension building in him. "Sorry you're caught in my web."

"I'm not," I say softly. And it's true.

If Armando hadn't killed a man in my shop last week, I wouldn't have the privilege of knowing him. Of knowing what it means to be possessed by a man like him.

And I wouldn't give that up for anything.

But his expression is blank, like the shooting tweaked

his PTSD. He just shakes his head. "I wanted you safe from all of this."

"Hey." I place my hand on his cheek, forcing him to look at me. "I am safe. And Marco will be okay too, Armando."

His dark eyes meet mine, and for a moment, I see something raw and vulnerable there. "I don't know what I'd do if that had been you, Hannah." He swallows hard. "I can't stand the thought of you getting hurt because of me."

"Everything's going to be fine. I'm fine. Marco soon will be."

Armando shakes his head. "Nothing is fine right now. But I'm going to make damn sure it will be."

Chapter Two

Armando

Hannah's colorful platform heels click against the sterile floors, echoing in the emergency room as she paces.

Leo sits with his ankle across his knee, his foot jiggling. "Have you told the don?" he asks.

I shake my head. "Not yet."

There was a time when I would go to Don G in a heartbeat. About everything. But I feel so disconnected from *La Famiglia* now.

Of course, I have to report this. I have to tell him what's happening. But I want to be able to tell him that I have it figured out when I do. That I have it in hand.

The trouble is, I'm so fucking far from having it in hand. I need answers, so I can finish this shit.

Especially because Hannah's involved now.

I can't have her hurt.

I glance at the clock. It's been hours since Marco was brought in, and the silence in this cold, white room is deafening.

"God, when will they tell us something?" I mutter under my breath, trying to contain my frustration and fear.

I brood in the corner of the room, apart from Hannah, fighting the urge to slam my fist into the wall. I imagine the scene of Marco taking the bullet meant for me over and over in my mind, a constant reminder that I am to blame. What if it had struck his heart? His head? Right now I'd be explaining to my aunt how her son died.

The thought makes me sick.

I wanted to feel something–anything–but not this.

Thank fuck Hannah wasn't hit.

"Damn it." I clench my fists. My gaze drifts to Hannah, her beautiful face etched with worry, and my chest tightens even more. If only I hadn't brought her into this world, into the chaos of my past, she wouldn't be here facing this danger.

"Armando." She walks over to me. "He's going to be okay. And it's not your fault."

I look away, unable to meet her eyes. How can she still be so fucking sweet after all this? After I've brought her nothing but trouble and pain?

"Stop blaming yourself," she pleads, her voice breaking as tears well up in her eyes. "You couldn't have known this would happen."

I stare down at her. I don't know how the fuck she can cry for me. I'm the walking dead, and she's an ocean of emotion.

"Couldn't I?" I ask bitterly, images of my past flashing before me. Every failed deal, every vengeful enemy—they all led to this moment. "You need to be safe."

"What I need is you," she whispers, reaching out to touch my hand.

"Need me?" I scoff, pulling my hand away as if her touch is scalding. "You don't know what you're asking for."

I catch the hurt in her gaze, and my guilt grows.

"Maybe not." She looks down at her feet before raising her eyes to meet mine again. "But I know that my feelings don't change for you just because of what happened in that alley."

Fuck. This girl. She's so much more than I deserve.

A nurse comes into the waiting room and addresses Leo and me. "He's out of surgery," she tells us. "We removed the bullet from his—"

I surge to my feet and head straight to the room without asking if we can see him. Hannah follows right behind me. Leo stays to listen to the nurse's report.

I just need to see with my own eyes that he's okay.

"Hey, guys," Marco calls out weakly from his hospital bed. "Apparently it was just a bullet to my ass. I always knew my ass looked good but never thought it'd be a literal target!" He chuckles as best he can, given the pain he's in.

I force a smile, appreciating his attempt to lighten the mood despite his own suffering. The sound of his laughter is like a balm to the heaviness in my chest. Though he tries to hide it, I see the strain on his face. It's evident that he's putting on a brave front for our sake.

"Nice one, *cugino*," I say with a half-smile.

"Come on, Hannah, you may not laugh at my jokes, but at least give me a smile." Marco gazes at her expectantly.

"Only because you're injured." Her smile could brighten the darkest prison cell.

"Hey, I'll take what I can get," he teases, wincing as he shifts on the bed.

"Thank you, Marco. For taking the bullet," I say sincerely.

"Yes, thank you," Hannah adds. "I know it could have hit me. You saved my life."

"Anytime." He shrugs. "I've been in this life long enough to know the risks. I'm not some innocent bystander who got caught up in your mess, Armando. I made my choices."

Despite Marco's words, guilt gnaws at me like a ravenous wolf. I clench my fists at my sides and look away from them, trying to fight the urge to rage and kill someone.

"Marco shouldn't have been there," I say, my voice strained. "It should've been me in that alley. The bullet was meant for me."

"Armando, you can't—" Hannah begins, but she's cut off by the sudden entrance of Marco's brother, Leo.

"What the hell happened?" Leo saunters into the hospital room.

"I got shot in the butt."

"So I heard." Leo barks out a laugh. "Well, at least it wasn't something important."

"Ha, very funny." Marco gives a rueful grin. "I did what I had to do."

"So now you have two holes in your ass?" Leo continues. "So you are a double asshole now."

"Keep it up, little brother," Marco growls.

"Listen," I interject, addressing Leo. "This is my mess. I'll make it right. I promise." The weight of responsibility settles even more heavily on my shoulders. I glance over at Hannah, who studies me like she can feel it. I'm sure she can. The girl feels everything.

I can't read her thoughts.

Leo stops joking with Marco and turns toward me. "Count me in, on finding the fuckers who scarred my brother's lily-white ass." Leo's face is serious. "We'll make sure they regret ever crossing our family."

As we discuss plans for retribution, Marco interjects, wincing as he adjusts his position on the bed.

"Before you guys go all vigilante on their asses, there's something we need to consider." He tips his head in Hannah's direction. "Maybe it's best if she gets out of town for a while, too. Like your mom."

"Absolutely not," Hannah responds immediately, her voice unwavering.

Fuck. Marco's right. If anyone connects me to Hannah, she'll be a target. The *stronzos* who want me dead were in the alleyway behind her shop today. They may have already tied me to her.

Then again, it could be they thought I'd be there because of Rocco's. Because it's where they found me last time.

Hannah puts her hands on her hips. "No. I have a business to run. I'm not going anywhere."

I'm a double-asshole because the truth is, I don't want her to leave. I don't want to stop hiding out at her place. I don't want to let her go. She's the only color in my black and white life.

"I don't think she's a target. Just me."

"True. I heard them yelling 'that's not him' after they shot me," Marco says.

A small sliver of relief worms its way through my chest. "That's good. Hannah stays, then."

She steps in close to me, and I wrap my arms around her, pulling her close, inhaling the scent of her hair—a mixture of fresh flowers and warm vanilla.

"You stay, but we'll need to take extra precautions."

"Okay," she murmurs, her arms tightening around me.

"All right, then," Leo chimes in, his expression still serious. "We'll make sure to keep her safe while you deal with this. And I'll help you handle the retribution, Armando."

"Hey, don't forget about me," Marco calls out, attempting a grin despite the pain etched on his face. "I might be down, but I'm not out. I'll be back on my feet soon. The retribution should be mine." He yawns. "But right now, I need to close my eyes and enjoy the high from all these pain meds."

Leo leans against the wall as he crosses his arms over his chest. "Yeah, man, and now you're gonna have all the nurses here fighting over who gets to change your bandages."

"Maybe I should get shot more often, huh?" Marco chuckles, wincing slightly from the effort.

"Maybe not in the butt next time, though. Takes the cool factor out of the equation," I quip, earning a laugh from everyone in the room.

"All right, All right, enough with the jokes," Marco says, catching his breath. "But seriously, Mando, promise me you won't go off on your own for this one. We're a team, remember?"

"Yeah." The room falls silent as I nod, holding Marco's gaze. "I promise." I take Hannah's hand and lead her out of the hospital room. "Let's go home."

Chapter Three

Armando

"We need to get you in the shower." I nudge Hannah to the bathroom in her apartment.

When my hand reaches the small of her back, I feel a tremble. Fuck. She's probably still in shock.

I hate seeing the blood on her. Though it isn't hers, it still makes me sick to my stomach imagining what could have been if Marco wasn't there to take the bullet.

I guide her into the shower, turning on the water and adjusting the temperature until it's warm but not too hot. She stands there, eyes closed, steam rising around her as the water cascades down her body. I can see the tension in her shoulders start to ease as she relaxes, and for a moment, I allow myself to let go of the dread that's been gripping me since I found her and Marco in the alley.

She closes her eyes and tilts her head back, letting the water soak into her hair. I reach for the body wash and lather it up in my hands before gently massaging it along her bare flesh.

"Are you okay?" I croak. "Really okay?"

She nods, the tension leaving her body. She's safe, at least for now. I know I can't stay in her life much longer. Not when I'm putting her through this kind of shit.

"It's okay," I murmur, "I won't let you be involved in anything else. I promise."

Twenty-four hours ago, there would be no way possible I could simply bathe this woman and not want to thrust my cock up inside of her. Soapy water streaming down her dark skin has my dick hardening, but I focus on my goal. Right now, all I want to do is soothe her. Wrap her in a fluffy blanket and chase away all her monsters.

Once she's clean, I help her out of the shower and wrap her in a towel. I lead her to the bedroom and help her into a fresh pair of pajamas before tucking her into bed.

"I'm fine, Armando," she insists again.

I sit beside her, unable to think of anything but the shooting. The blood pooling under Marco. He took a bullet for Hannah. I know he'd do it again in a heartbeat.

She shouldn't be involved in any of this. Shouldn't have seen me choke the life out of a man on her shop floor. Shouldn't have been shot at in the alleyway.

She's an innocent, and we don't involve innocents. Especially not women.

Fuck. I stand. "Get some sleep," I say gruffly.

She grabs my hand to stop me. "Don't go. Come to bed with me."

Oh, the temptation. She's looking at me with those big, brown eyes. So beautiful in her bed.

But she doesn't need sex right now. She needs comfort.

I kick off my pants and climb into bed beside her, and she snuggles into my chest, her hand resting on my heart. The rise and fall of her breaths are soothing.

I lie there and stare up at the ceiling, my mind chewing on the day's events.

I shouldn't have let myself get close to this girl. I feel I'm signing her death certificate.

Being with me is the same as walking toward the Reaper himself.

Fuck, I should leave...

"What happens now?"

I don't have the answer to that. All I know is that I can't keep putting her in danger. I can't keep this up forever. "I don't know," I admit. "But I'll figure it out. I won't let anything happen to you. Whoever shot at you and Marco is going to die. I'm going to tear his head off with my bare hands."

I feel her tense.

"Sorry." I should definitely spare her the details of my revenge plan. "What I mean is, what happened today will never happen again."

She gives a wobbly nod. Her gaze doesn't reveal any fear or revulsion for me. No, this is the girl who watched me kill a man with my bare hands and still kissed me.

I lean in and taste her mouth.

As her lips part, I deepen the kiss, exploring the sweet depths of her mouth with my tongue. She responds to me, her body pressing against mine with increasing urgency. Our breathing becomes ragged as we continue to kiss, lost in the intoxicating sensation of each other's touch.

I slide my hands down her back, pulling her in closer to me. Her breasts press against my chest, and a moan escapes her lips.

I pull away for a moment to catch my breath, looking into her eyes as I run my hand through her hair. We're lost in each other, and the world outside of this moment doesn't exist. I lean in to kiss her again, and I climb on top, my hands roaming over her body as I kiss her deeply. She responds with fervor, her hips grinding against mine. I can feel her wetness through her panties and makes my cock rock hard.

We both slowly remove the rest of our clothing, not wanting anything to prevent our skins from merging as one.

I trail kisses down her body, starting with her neck, continuing down to her breasts and then further down to the soft patch of dark hair between her thighs. I kiss her softly at first, and then I part her lips with my tongue and plunge in, tasting her.

She lets out a gasp, her hands grabbing onto my head as she arches her back. I continue exploring, my tongue darting with quick flicks as I lap up her juices. She gasps again, letting out a high pitched moan as she claws at my hair.

I part her thighs wider with my hands, running my tongue slowly through her folds. She shudders in response.

"Oh God." She lets out a shaky breath.

I slide my arms underneath her thighs, pulling her legs up to my shoulders. Her breathing quickens as my tongue flicks against her clit. She digs her nails into my back, arching as I lick her slowly, my tongue brushing over her sensitive nub. Her body tenses up as I flick faster, her muscles tightening as I push her closer and closer to the edge.

I continue my assault on her clit, running my tongue around it in tight circles. Alternating between licking and sucking as I hear her breathing deepen and grow shaky.

"I'm going to come," she mumbles. Her entire body is trembling now, her muscles tensing up and releasing in a powerful orgasm. Her juices flow into my mouth as she moans loudly.

I continue until she's done, finally sitting up and looking at her. She's breathing heavily, her chest rising and falling quickly. She wraps her arms around my neck, pulling me into a kiss.

I grab a condom from the bedside table. I tear the wrapping open with my teeth and slide the condom on. I lift her legs back up to my shoulders, looking deep into her eyes as I enter her with a single thrust. We both gasp, lost in the sensation of our bodies joining together. I pull out and thrust into her again. I pull back and thrust a third time, each thrust growing more and more powerful.

She pulls my head to her and kisses me, her lips meeting mine in a powerful, soulful kiss as we continue to make love to each other.

Not just fucking. Making love. My penance for all I've put her through.

She breaks the kiss, pressing her forehead against mine, and we continue to move together in unison. Her breath is hot against my face. My own desire builds, and I start to thrust harder and deeper into her. I begin to feel the familiar tingling sensation in my groin as she continues to moan and whimper, her breath getting more and more ragged. We're both nearing the edge now, and she tightens her legs around my waist as her breath quickens. I thrust into her one last time. We explode in a series of moans and groans, riding the wave together until it breaks. I slowly slide out of her, lying beside her in the bed. We're both trying to catch our breaths.

She turns to me, snuggling up to my heated body. I wrap my arm around her, holding her close to me. Despite the shitshow of the day, this feels right.

Being here, with Hannah. This connection.

Yet, this is the exact thing I need to give up if I care about this girl.

As she rests her head on my chest again, I can feel her body relax and her breathing grow slow and steady. Her eyes close, and I know that she's finally given in to the exhaustion that's threatened to overwhelm her since I found her in the alley.

I lie here, holding her close, and I can't help but think of how ironic it is that the one woman I should keep at arm's length is the one woman I can't bring myself to let go of.

Chapter Four

Hannah

I wake in Armando's arms. The room is dark, his heavy breathing tells me he's been asleep for awhile.

I should be scared of this man. Terrified of the situation I am in. I don't even know how to define my relationship with Armando. Am I still his prisoner? His girlfriend?

Is he only here because he needs a place to hide out? Is he still making sure I won't rat him out?

Or does he want to be here? With me?

The foolish part of me likes to believe I'm doing something for him. A shock absorber in his messy, criminal life.

I know that's totally fucked up, but there it is. I want to be important to him. I want to know he needs me like I'm starting to need him.

His arms tighten around me. His grip is possessive, as if he's still afraid I'll run.

It feels like a lifetime since he literally crashed into my shop.

So much fear. Unknown. Pleasure. Lust. Even tenderness.

Yes, tenderness from the killer in my bed.

Now, as I lie here in his arms, I can't help but feel a strange sense of comfort. It's as if I'm finally safe from the world outside. The world that would judge me for being here. The world that doesn't understand the bond that has formed between us.

Do I even understand the bond?

I turn to look at him, and he stirs in his sleep. His eyes open, and he smiles when he sees me looking at him. I feel a warmth spread through my body. It's crazy, I know. But I can't help how I feel. I love him. I know I shouldn't, but I do.

"Can't sleep?" he murmurs, pulling me closer.

I shake my head, unable to find the words to express what I feel. I just stare at him, and he stares back, his eyes searching my face for something. He leans in and brushes his lips against mine, sending shivers down my spine. I respond eagerly, pressing my body against his.

In that moment, I forget everything that surrounds us. The hit out on Armando. The shooting in the alley. The threat of Armando breaking parole and ending back in prison.

I break the kiss, pulling back just enough so my fingers can trace light circles on his chest. "Just thinking," I whisper back, unwilling to break the spell of the moment.

He nods, his eyes searching mine. "About what?"

"About how close I feel to you. And what's going to happen."

He's silent for a moment, his expression inscrutable. "I don't have the answers, Flowers. I don't know."

"I know," I say quickly. "Of course you don't. Nevermind."

"I do know one thing..." His hand moves towards my thigh.

My breath catches in my throat when I feel his fingers brush against my leg. My skin is covered with goose bumps, my body responding to his touch.

I open my legs wider in an attempt to get his fingers closer to my pussy.

He lowers his hand to the edge of my panties. "You're a gift."

Every cell in my body celebrates his admission. Confirmation that I do mean something. That I am a contribution to his life. That he does need me.

"You're a fucking gift, and I want you more than I've ever wanted you before." His fingers slide under the fabric and find my swollen clit. I gasp, his touch sending a jolt through my body.

My whole body quivers in anticipation as he slides a finger inside of me. He pushes it deep inside, pumping it in and out in a rhythmic motion. My body knows what to do. It knows how to respond to his touch. It's been like this since the moment I met him.

"Thank you for accepting me." He strokes my inner walls. "I love the way you surrender to me. It's intoxicating. I can never get enough of you." He inhales the scent of my hair. "Never."

I've come to realize that Armando and I may struggle for words as we are just learning how to communicate. But one thing is for certain.

Our bodies know how to speak.

More so than words.

I let out a soft moan as his finger slides in and out of my pussy, "More," I whisper, my eyes never leaving his.

"More?" His lips curl into a smile.

"I want more than this. I want you inside of me. I need you," I admit, my voice catching in my throat.

I've never been one who could easily express my sexual needs and desires. But when I'm around him, he brings out a side of me that I never knew existed.

A side that craves his touch.

"I know what you need, Flowers." He rolls me to my back and pins my forearms by my sides.

"Yes," I breathe, thrilled by his dominance.

"You need me to fuck you?"

"Yes," I answer immediately.

"You need me to fuck you hard, baby girl?"

"Yes, please."

"You're asking for it." He reaches down to grab my panties and pulls them down my legs. He tosses them on the floor, then grabs my ankles and lifts my legs towards the headboard. I squirm in pleasure as he spreads my legs apart, exposing my pussy to his hungry gaze.

"You're so fucking wet for me," he growls as he lowers his head, pressing his lips against my thigh, then moving towards my pussy. "So wet and ready for me, aren't you?"

He doesn't wait for an answer. His lips land on my clit, and he sucks it between his lips. His warm tongue flicks over my clit, torturing it in a most delicious way.

I squeeze my eyes shut, warmth spreading through my body as a bolt of electricity shoots up my spine. I gasp as he pushes his tongue deep inside of me, groaning as it slides against my swollen clit. His tongue pushes inside of me, and my pussy contracts, quivering against his mouth.

He pushes two fingers inside of me, and my pussy contracts around them. I'm so close. "Put it in me," I breathe, struggling to find my voice.

"Put what in you?" His fingers plunge even deeper, driving me wild. He's making me beg.

I oblige. "Your cock. I want it. I need it."

"Nice and slow?" he asks.

"Yes," I nod.

"Are you sure? Or do you want it rough and hard?" he teases.

"However you want. I just want you to fuck me." My heart pounds in my chest. The blood sizzles through my veins.

I've never had an addictive personality. I don't drink. I don't smoke. Nothing has ever taken hold of my senses.

Until Armando.

I'm completely addicted to him.

And I'm terrified he's going to break my heart.

Chapter Five

Hannah

The sun spills through the thin curtains of my small apartment, casting a soft glow on the room.

I hear water running in the shower, and knowing Armando is still here calms me.

I get up and flit aimlessly around the bedroom, picking up strewn clothing without thinking. No, that's not true. I'm *trying* not to think, but yesterday's events are playing on loop in my mind. The sudden screech of tires, the sharp crack of gunfire, and Marco's pained eyes haunt me.

Someone wants Armando dead.

That thought terrifies me. I stare at the floor, searching for answers that aren't there.

As if on cue, the bathroom door creaks open, and Armando strides out, his damp hair slicked back from his face. He's dressed impeccably in a tailored suit, looking every bit the powerful and dangerous man he is. It's as if last night never happened, like he's untouchable. As always, his presence is both reassuring and intimidating.

"Morning, Flowers," he says coolly, eyes scanning me from head to toe. His voice is like velvet, soothing some of the anxiety that has been gnawing at me since I woke up. But his stoic demeanor also serves as a reminder that this kind of violence isn't new to him—it's part of his life.

"Morning," I reply, trying to steady my voice. "How's Marco?"

"Alive," he answers simply, his expression still as calm and collected as ever. "He'll be fine. It's not the first time he's been shot." There's a hint of bitterness in his words, daring me to question him further. But I can't help myself.

"Did he say how long he'll be in the hospital? I was thinking of sending him some flowers."

"Don't. I don't want you to be seen with him. Or me. I don't want that connection made for anyone. Okay?"

"Is this what your life will always be like? Are we constantly going to be in danger?"

His eyes flash with something dark, almost vulnerable, before he turns away. "There is no *we*, Hannah," he says quietly, his back to me. "*Because* of the danger. I'm sorry you got dragged into this, but I'm going to try to keep you out of anything else."

Right. No *we*.

Armando turns, and he must see my hurt because he moves to me, wraps his arms around me, and pulls me close. My face presses against his chest, the steady rhythm of his heart beating beneath my ear. It's comforting, grounding me in this moment.

"I'm sorry I got you into this." His voice is tense, but his fingers trace my back gently.

"I think the adrenaline of last night is wearing off. I feel... scared," I confess, my hands gripping the fabric of his suit jacket. "Not for me, but for you."

He lets out a shocked chuff. "Me? Don't worry about me, baby girl. The outfit... it's a part of me. Danger is woven into every day for me. That won't change. I can't give it up, even if I wanted to." His voice cracks slightly, betraying the pain he feels in admitting this truth.

"Is this who you are then? A man constantly surrounded by violence and fear?" I ask, trying to understand the depth of his involvement in the mafia but also hoping I don't sound judgey.

"Unfortunately, yes," he admits, his grip on me tightening. "I was born into this life, and I've done things I'm not proud of. But I don't want it to touch you any more than it already has, Hannah. You deserve better."

My eyes swim with tears.

I know he's saying he cares about me, but he's also pushing me away. Shutting me out. Telling me we have no future.

"Just because I'm scared–" I stop. I'm not sure what to say. "Armando, I don't care about your past or what you are."

He seems to stop breathing. "You should." His voice is hard. Dark.

"I know what I deserve. And right now, that's you."

My chest tightens at the thought of a future filled with violence and fear, but I can't imagine my life without him in it. I know it's not his fault that he was born into this world, and I don't want to ask him to change who he is. However, I can't ignore the fact that by being with him, I'm accepting a life that may never be free from danger.

Facing that reality doesn't mean I have to flee from it.

"I promise you, I'll do everything in my power to keep you safe. What happened yesterday will not go unpunished. I'll make damn sure none of this touches you again."

Armando's jaw tightens, and I see the fierce protectiveness rising within him.

He looks at me for a long moment, the weight of his past heavy in his gaze. His breath warm against my skin. Something shifts in his expression then, a spark igniting behind his eyes.

* * *

Armando

I take the L to the construction site and check in with the foreman, Larry. He gives me the up and down. I dressed in a suit and tie, which I know is overdressed for a construction site. But it's not overdressed for a lieutenant of the mafia, and I need to establish who the fuck I am.

"Yeah. Okay. So on the books you're listed as a supervisor. If anyone ever shows up here to inspect, just look official. You dressed the part, so that's good. Other than that—you do what you want. I'm sure you know that already."

I nod. "Yeah. Definitely. So am I supposed to be your supervisor?"

His nostrils flare. "That's right. Real supervisor manages eight other sites. I handle everything here on my own."

I shove my hands in my pockets to look less threatening. Not a look I've perfected, but somewhere in me, there used to be a guy who knew how to do casual. "So maybe I'll just tag along with you... learn the ropes."

What else am I gonna do? I spent four and a half years bored. Now that I'm out, I don't want to lounge around and do nothing. Plus, I need something to keep my mind off the thought of Hannah almost getting shot. That and our night and morning of epic fucking.

Of course, Larry doesn't like that. Not one fucking bit. I know because he kinda goes stiff and freezes for a couple seconds before he lets out a choked, "Yeah, okay."

He has to say *okay*. No one's gonna fuck with me here. The Pachino family runs the union.

I follow him around and pay attention, introducing myself to the guys when Larry doesn't bother. It's not that I suddenly feel friendly. Fuck no. But I force myself to at least go through the motions.

"He's the union-provided supervisor," Larry inserts meaningfully each time, letting them all know exactly what that means.

I'm a mobster there to milk their employer for a paycheck while doing nothing.

Well, they might be surprised. I might end up doing more than texting my buddies all day. Or I might not. Who the fuck knows? All I know is I'm hungry to work. I had to hold myself back from inserting myself into Hannah's business. Telling her all the ideas I had for it.

That would be wrong. Hannah doesn't need me to bust in and tell her how to do anything. She's gotta figure that shit out on her own, or else she'll never take full ownership over there. But damn, I want to help.

A big black guy in his fifties comes over to talk to Larry. When I introduce myself, I find out his name is Harold, and he's an electrician.

I can tell he doesn't want to say what he is about to. "Listen, I've been a little short of breath lately, and my wife got me an appointment this afternoon with one of her doctors at the hospital. I know it's short notice, and we're on a deadline, but—"

"No way, Harold. Absolutely not. You know we have to get the wiring up today or the inspection won't pass."

I don't know if I'm dicking with Larry or just want to throw my weight around, but I interject. Afterall, I'm technically his boss, right? "Let him finish," I say. "Maybe he has a plan to make sure it all gets done." I turn my gaze on Harold. "Do you?"

"Yeah," he says. I can hear the piss-off in his voice. "I was going to say that I should be finished by lunch time, and if anything comes up in the inspection, Chad can handle it."

"Chad can't handle something this important. No way," Larry splutters. It's possible he's just pissed that I inserted myself. Or maybe he's always a dick. Larry's in his late thirties. Good looking. Probably has a pretty wife and kid at home.

I already want to bust his teeth in, and I'm sure he feels the same way about me for sticking my nose in the business.

"Short of breath sounds serious," I say. "You'd better keep that appointment."

Eat my shit, Larry.

Larry's face turns deep red.

"If something comes up during the inspection that Chad can't handle, can we call your cell?" I pull out my phone.

Harold appears relieved. "Of course." He gives me his number while Larry shifts from foot to foot, looking like he's getting anally fisted.

Probably not my brightest move pissing off the foreman on my first day. Then again, these fuckers can't touch me. Not that I need the organization's back in this situation, but the Pachino's have instilled enough fear in Local 352 over the past 30 years that no one in his right mind would even say *boo* to me.

And I'm already a shred closer to enjoying myself. I guess the alpha male in me needed to piss on someone. Plus,

I know I'm right. Why the fuck would a foreman deny a guy short of breath from a semi-emergency doctor's visit? That's fucked up.

"Show me who Chad is," I instruct Harold and follow him further into the building.

I'm gonna make this job my bitch. Because right now, it's the only thing I have.

Unless I count Hannah. I mean, I definitely count Hannah, but I can't really consider her mine. Yeah, I claimed her right from the fucking start. And she definitely went with it.

But I have jack shit to offer her. I can't be her boyfriend. Not when there's a gang shooting up my apartment, a murder attempt on my cousin, and I'm an emotional carcass.

She deserves better than that.

Which means... fuck. I probably should leave her the hell alone. Make a clean break before she gets hurt.

Only I'm way too fucking selfish right now to do that.

Because that girl is about the only thing that brings me light right now.

Chapter Six

Hannah

At 5:30 pm, I clean up. I actually told Josie to leave early because there was nothing to do, and having her around made me anxious.

I'm still anxious even with her gone. A different feeling though. This one doesn't have that Josie signature on it.

It has Armando's.

Because I'm trying to figure out what to do. Do I call him to ask when he'll be home? I actually don't even think I have his phone number, which is lame. Will he be at my house when I return? He should be. He left a duffel bag of clothes there.

But what if he's not?

Why did he leave this morning? He said he had to work, but I don't even know what he does. He is the least forthcoming person I've ever known.

Probably because he has the most to hide.

Not that I think he was off robbing banks this morning or anything, but you never know. He's in the mafia. It could be anything.

The memory of him grappling with the guy trying to kill him flashes through my mind. His calm but deadly offensive. He was magnificent. Is it weird that I'm not overly bothered by his career or what he's done? And there was a shooting yesterday that, yes, rattled me, but oddly, I'm already over it. I should be terrified, but I'm not. It could be due to the suited men standing outside my shop all day, but the fear I had this morning has mostly dissipated.

The only true emotion I've had all day is longing. I miss Armando.

To me, the danger just makes Armando all the more appealing. He's the bad boy who lives by a code. There's honor to him. He's killed, yes, but it was in battle. Like a soldier.

Only his army is a Sicilian family, not a government troop.

Maybe I'm trying to rationalize it all, but the fact remains—I can't muster many misgivings about it. Because I like the way it feels to be consumed by him.

And that's when he walks in my front door.

My heart skips to the jingle of the bells. He looks sharp in a suit jacket and slacks, one hand shoved casually in his pocket.

I freeze, breath caught at having him in here again. He strides right over to me without a word, grips the back of my head and stares down.

"Hey," I breathe.

His gaze roves over my face, examining the nose jewelry he gave me as a gift right before Marco was shot. I forgot to thank him for it with all that happened.

"Pretty." A man of few words.

And then he kisses me. It's not the desperate sort of kiss we've engaged in—the kind where he consumes me, and I burst into flames. This kiss is more sensual. Like a Hollywood movie kiss. The kind at the end of the film where the guy gets the girl, the music swells and the camera circles around them.

I don't lift my arms, I just leave them dangling at my sides, loving the feeling of receiving what he's delivering. Letting him take what he wants without trying for more.

When he breaks the kiss, the shop spins in that panning camera feel, and he looks down at me and at the nose ring. "You like it?"

I find my breath. "I love it." And then, stupid me, my eyes fill with tears. Because, as usual, I make the gift mean way more than it probably does. "I meant to thank you before. But with everything that happened to Marco, I—"

He kisses me again. Hard. Claiming.

He's unmoved by the tears. Not in a bad way, but he doesn't react at all, just keeps looking down at me like he's trying to peer into my soul.

"What are you thinking?" I ask. Because I desperately need to get into his head right now.

"I'm trying to figure out if I should take you home to wear out your bed or take you to dinner." My expression must reveal my pleasure because he says, "You want dinner, huh?"

I actually don't care which he picks, I'm just looking forward to being with him, but a date does sound nice. I reach for him, looping my arms around his neck and initiating a kiss.

And then it's on. His dark hunger rears again, and his kiss and touch turn aggressive. He slides his hands up my dress, squeezing my ass, and his fingers are in my panties in the next breath.

I'm already wet. Maybe I was the moment he walked in

that door. My body seems to belong to him. He commands it, and all I want to do is give it over to him.

But this is all so dangerous. I'm in way over my head. Any day now I'm going to figure out that he has no intention of continuing with me.

And dammit—isn't that just the insanity of relationships? You don't get a guarantee the other person wants the same thing you do. You just hope and wish and do your best as you fumble through. And yeah, it's messy. Yeah, it usually ends with a broken dream.

This probably will too. I try to remind myself at every breath, and it creates a riot of anxiety mingled with the pleasure that he hasn't left yet, which sadly only heightens the experience.

He's still dangerous to me, only now, it's in a far worse way.

I'm going to lose my heart to him.

He drags his open mouth along my neck and bites me. "You gonna let me fuck you in your shop again?" His voice is rough, a low growl. "Let off steam, so I can make it through dinner?"

Like he would have blue balls if we don't have sex first. Like he needs me that badly. It's a powerful feeling to be that wanted—I've never experienced it before.

"What do you think?" I want more words out of this guy. Find out if his thoughts match the feelings I absorb from him.

"I think you are." He steps back and unbuckles his belt.

My eyes track the movement, finding it slightly threatening and extremely hot.

"Oh, you want the belt?"

Shit! Do I? Definitely not. Only... heat floods between my legs.

He loops the belt around my waist and uses it to pull my hips against his body. "Tell me, *bella*, how do you want my belt?"

A shiver runs through my body at the thought of him using it to spank me. Do I want *that*? I don't think so, but my body disagrees, my excitement level ratcheting even higher.

He continues talking as he backs me toward the door and locks it, turning my *Open* sign to *Closed*. "You want it around your throat while I fuck you from behind? Hmm?" His breath is hot on my ear. "Or should I use it to bind your wrists behind your back?"

Oh, damn. I hadn't considered either of those possibilities. And they both freak me out and turn me on in equal measures.

"Or did you just want to feel it across your ass?"

This time the shiver that runs through me is big enough for him to sense.

"Don't worry, Flowers. I'll make sure you like it."

He shifts the belt to loop under my ass and pulls up to pin our bodies together. My core is molten right now. We've barely gotten started, and I'm already losing my sanity. Close to orgasm.

This is what this man does to me.

It's crazy.

He spins me around and backs me into the break room. "I wanted you on your bed. On your forearms and knees with those thighs spread wide. Will you do that for me later, beautiful?"

"Yes," I swear. I'd promise him just about anything right now. I'm drunk with lust. Drunk on him.

He turns me around and pulls up the hem of my short cotton dress. "You always wear these short fucking dresses. They make me crazy, Flowers. Make it so easy for me to bare your ass and spank this pretty skin purple." The most this guy talks is when we're having sex. No wonder that's the place I feel like we connect best. He yanks my panties down and delivers four slaps to my ass, then rubs out the sting. "You're so hot. So beautiful."

Keep talking, boss man. His words are a balm to my ears. Maybe I *am* needy. Clingy. Whatever. Because I drink his praise right now like it's an elixir. But this guy doesn't talk much, so when he does, it feels significant.

"Spread," he commands, shoving my panties down until they drop to the floor. His voice is so deep and sure. I can't imagine anyone ever argues with him.

I widen my stance and hollow my back, emboldened by all his praise. He slides his belt between my legs and brings the leather over my core.

"Mmm," I moan.

He pulls it back out and flicks just the end of it between my legs, spanking my pussy.

I gasp. It stings, but he went lightly. It's not painful. Just a little hurty.

"You like getting your pussy spanked, little girl?"

Oh damn. Now he's calling me *little girl*. Why do I love that so much?

"N-no," I lie.

He replaces the belt with his fingers and rubs over my slit. I'm sopping wet. "I think you do. You want me to spank your ass with it?"

My breath is audible. Not quite a gasp, but a rasping between us. I don't answer.

"Hmm? I think you want to try it, don't you? Are you scared, Flowers?"

I nod my head up and down. I'm facing the Formica

table, the grey speckled surface swimming in front of my eyes.

He steps right up to me, kicks my legs wider, and cages my throat, pulling my torso up until my back meets his front. His hardened cock presses against my ass through his pants. "You like a little pain with your pleasure, don't you, Hannah? Or is it fear?"

Hot prickles skitter across my skin. I can already tell I'm going to bawl when this is over because there's pressure in my face, tears in my throat. His hand there amplifies the feeling. He's not squeezing, but he easily could. If those fingers tightened, he could end my life, just like that.

He's done it before, I'll bet.

Yeah, it's the danger. "Fear," I whisper. I feel things so intensely. When sex combines with danger, it amplifies everything.

He bites my ear. Not a nip, but a punishing bite that's almost too hard. "Are you afraid of what I'm going to do to you now?" He's wicked, taunting me like the devil teases his prey.

"Yeah."

"Three strokes," he murmurs and pushes my torso back down to the table.

I let out a whimper. I *am* scared. Scared it will hurt. Scared I'll embarrass myself with my reaction. Scared of being so vulnerable with this man who is quickly becoming so much to me.

"Then I'm going to fuck you good. And after I'm gonna treat you like a princess. *Capito?*"

Do I understand? Not even remotely.

But I am totally on board. A rush of adrenaline floods my veins as he steps back and winds one end of his belt around his fist.

Oh God. What am I getting myself into? This is crazy. Crazier than kissing a killer.

He whips the belt through the air. It lands across the lower portion of my buttocks leaving a line of fire. I gasp, clenching my cheeks together.

"Oh God." I try to straighten, but he holds me down.

"More?" He's letting me know I can stop this even though he's holding me down. I can't bring myself to ask for more. I'm not sure I want it. But I don't tell him to stop, either.

I leave it up to him.

And of course, he understands that. Despite how emotionally unavailable Armando may seem, he's pretty perceptive when it comes to my emotions. He does pay attention.

He whips me again, and I jump and let out a cry this time. He rubs over the two stripes, kneading the pain into a more generalized burning.

I moan softly.

"I said three. You gonna take the last one like a good girl?"

Checking in again.

"Yes." I bob my head, like promising to be good will make it any easier.

He slides his hand down and strokes between my legs. "Yes, you are a good girl, aren't you? Always so good."

I'm trembling all over. Feverish.

He plays with my clit, and I arch back, moaning. He grips my hips and leans over to kiss one of my burning buttcheeks. "One more," he says firmly as he rises.

Damn.

He swings, and I gasp, and then it's over. Armando's clothing rustles, and I hear the crackle of the condom wrapper. He drags the head of his cock through my juices. Finding me so ready, he feeds himself in.

I'm not sure penetration has ever been so satisfying as it is right now. The rightness of him filling me couldn't be more plain. Like my body was made to accept his. Like this is its purpose.

Armando groans. "You're perfect, Hannah. So perfect." He eases in, inch by inch, then slowly backs out, teasing me with his length.

He may require the warm-up, but I don't. I'm ready for him to pound hard. Bruise my hips again or pull my hair. Instead, he slides his hands up my sides, inside my dress and dips his fingers into my bra to pinch one nipple.

I press my hands flat on the table and arch up, lifting my head. "Don't tease me," I tell him. Need's made me cranky now. "I need to finish."

He answers with a hard slam home. "That what you want, beautiful? Nice hard fuck? 'Cause that always suits me."

He bands an arm around my waist, careful to protect my hips from the table this time, and starts jackhammering into me.

"Yes," I moan, satisfaction looming close.

He plants one hand beside mine for leverage and plows into me, his loins slapping my ass, grinding in the burn from his belt, smoothing it out, satisfying it.

"I love you."

Oh shit. Why the fuck did I say that? I definitely didn't mean to. These things always come out of my mouth! I mean, it's true. In this moment, the love is flowing, *but Jesus!*

Why did I have to say it?

He falters, breaking rhythm, and I'm sure this is going to end badly.

Like maybe the worst of all endings because this time I'm freaking head over heels for this guy.

But instead of getting awkward and weird, he gets more aggressive. He fists my hair and pulls my head back sharply, sending a thousand tiny prickles of pain across my scalp.

"You love it when I fuck you hard, don't you, *bella*?" he growls, like he's mad at me. Like he's saying the words between clenched teeth.

"Yes!" I cry out, relieved at how he twisted my words. How he ran with it.

"You're going to like it when I fuck this ass, too."

Oh God. I almost laugh out loud. Maybe that's what love means to him. Anal.

"Harder," I urge him on, wanting to get to my finish, but maybe also trying to rush past my mistake.

He keeps pounding into me, giving it the way I like. Loving me back with that big cock of his.

"I need you."

Oh my God, my mouth won't stop.

He pulls tighter on my hair. "I'll give it to you," he growls. And he does. Even harder. Hard enough I'm getting sore. Wonderfully brutal. Like a beast released from his cage.

And then I scream. I come hard as he gets rougher and rougher with me.

He comes, and when he's done, reaches around to rub my clit and gets a second orgasm out of me.

And now that it's over, I wish we were in bed where I could collapse my face into a pillow and pretend I fell asleep.

Chapter Seven

Armando

She loves me. It's another of those moments where I'm sure I should feel more than I do. But I'm blank.

I mean, I'm not stupid enough to believe all the babble that comes out of a girl's mouth when she's about to orgasm, but I also know Hannah's an open book. She felt love for me in that moment and couldn't keep the secret.

And despite my lack of reaction to the words, I am changed by them.

Only problem is, I can tell she's embarrassed and wishing she hadn't said it.

She's also trembly as hell. I feel her legs wobbling where our thighs meet. I clean us both up and help her get back into her panties.

She avoids eye contact. "Hey, I hope you don't listen to all the crazy stuff I say during sex," she says in a rush.

"Nah, I'm taking it," I tell her, leading her out of the break room and shutting off the lights. "It's been a long time since I've heard that shit."

I shouldn't call it *shit*—that was a poor choice of words. But I'm trying to minimize the importance of it while still appreciating.

She shoots me a slightly tortured look that takes me aback. "Are you upset over her? Your fiancée?"

Oh.

She's jealous. *That* I experience viscerally. Like pleasure straight through my chest.

Hannah's claiming me.

Except I shouldn't like it. Because I can't be her boyfriend. Even if I didn't have an entire gang trying to kill me, I'm not boyfriend material. I'm the walking dead. I have nothing to offer a girl like Hannah—except for great sex. She's bright, vibrant. Has the whole world in front of her. She deserves everything.

I don't want to have this conversation. Like I'd rather pry off a toenail with pliers than talk about Grace, but Hannah's hanging out in the wind, vulnerability making her lick her lips and dart her gaze around.

So I stop in the darkened hallway and face her. "Grace is a cunt. No loyalty whatsoever. When I went to jail, she replaced me in weeks—fucking weeks—with another wiseguy. Didn't have the nerve to tell me for months, though."

Hannah cocks her head. "Does *wiseguy* mean another... guy in the organization?"

"Yeah. Emilio. He's like a cousin. Not a real fucking cousin but like one, you know?"

She stops breathing. I sound a little angry, which pisses me off. I want to go back to feeling nothing about it.

"When I got out last week, everyone thought there would be trouble. Me and him, you know? I used to be..." I don't even want to say it. What I used to be. Cocky. Self-assured. Proud. I don't even know that guy any more. "I don't know. Really fucking alpha dog. And I could be brutal. But you've seen that." I wince a little, thinking of what she saw here at her shop. I'm still amazed she showed no signs of trauma from it.

"The don warned me first thing not to touch it."

Hannah's worry has only increased. I swear to fuck, I'm catching her empath thing because even though I have no emotions of my own, I register hers clearly.

"But the thing they don't know is... I'm not that guy anymore. None of them fucking know me anymore. And I don't give a rat's ass about either of them. I mean, I'm disgusted by that shit—their lack of honor and loyalty—but it means nothing to me. Honestly, you know what would've been worse?"

"What?" Hannah whispers, eyes round.

I draw a breath, only just now realizing what I'm about to say. "If she'd waited for me."

It's true. If I'd had to get out and be expected to be the perfect boyfriend again—to live with Grace and plan our wedding together—I'd be cracking into pieces.

"I can't imagine having to marry her when I got out. Because I'm not the same guy who put the ring on her finger."

"But you would have?" Hannah asks.

I'm not sure what she's getting at or why she keeps picking this scab, but I answer honestly. "Yeah. I mean, I'd give her an out if she wanted it, but I don't break my commitments." I shrug. "I'm a man of my word."

She studies me with those warm brown eyes that see everything and never seem to judge. "You're loyal," she says.

I nod. "Always." I lead her out the alleyway door to the van. I open the passenger side and help her in. "Aw, hey. I forgot to check the mousetraps. You get any visitors?"

She cringes. "Yes."

"Are they still there? Need me to take care of them?"

More cringing. "Yes, please."

I give her a quick nod and go back inside to take care of it. Simple fucking thing for me to do for her. I'm glad there's something.

When I get back, I start the van. "Where do you want to go to dinner?"

"It's up to you, you're buying." She gives me an impish look. She likes when I pay. I used to be rolling in dough before I got picked up. If I still had that kind of money, I would flash it all over for her.

As it is, I'm doing okay. I have half the startup cash the don gave me, and I'll get a paycheck for a couple grand every two weeks. I'm not rich, but I can take a girl out for a nice dinner, for sure.

"You pick." I can't go anywhere I used to go. Hannah's place is still my safest hideout.

"Okay, um... I know a place."

Before I pull out, I pause and look at her. Really look at her. I don't want to just push her jealousy or concern about Grace aside, but I also don't want to discuss Grace anymore. "You're beautiful, you know that?"

Her eyes widen, her smile grows, and I can see she appreciates the compliment. I'm not good with words, but for her, I'll try. Every fucking day, I'll try.

"I've never had the privilege of being with a more beautiful woman before. Truly stunning," I add.

Chapter Eight

Armando

Hannah directs me to an artsy cafe. Not fancy but not a dive either. Industrial look with the no-ceiling thing where you can see all the ductwork above your head and the one hundred-year-old bricks in the walls. They don't have hard liquor, but the waiter brings us a bottle of wine to share.

I order a burger that comes with sweet potato fries instead of regular ones. She orders a fancy salad—beet pistachio or some shit like that. I watch her pleasure digging in and want to take her out to eat every night. She deserves to be treated way more than she treats herself.

"So what work did you have to do today?" she asks after the waiter disappears.

My instinct is to just clam up and not talk. Go silent on her, but I took her to dinner. We're on a goddamn date, so I shake my head. "Don't ask about my work."

The words are too hard. Too harsh. I can tell they didn't land right by how stiff she gets.

"It's for your safety, Hannah," I try to explain. "We don't talk business, not even with our women."

She studies me for a beat. "Am I your woman?"

I drain my glass of wine and refill it. Fuck. I am so not up for relationship talk. "I don't have a label for you, Flowers."

She fidgets, going silent, and a twinge of something moves around in my chest. What is it? Guilt? For being such a bad fucking date?

I search my brain for something to say and finally land on, "How was your day?"

Her mouth turns down. "Slow. But Tuesdays are always slow." She butters one of the mini muffins they brought in a bread basket. "I'm still working on what you said. Just trying new things." She takes a sip of wine.

"Yeah?" I encourage.

"Yeah. I have some ideas."

I lean forward. "Good. That's good. Like what?"

She shrugs, flushing a little. "A lot of ideas. I don't know which ones are good or where to start."

"You never do."

"I finally started an Instagram account and posted some of my favorite creations on it. Josie's been telling me forever to get on there."

Instagram. There's all this new social media shit out since I went in the pen. I guess I'd heard of Instagram before I went in, but I haven't been on it. I nod, making a mental note to check it out and check out her account. "That's great."

"There's this competition in a couple months. An arrangement contest. Mary Alice got second place in it once. I mean, I don't think it would directly translate to business, but it might help build my reputation. For people who don't trust the business with Mary Alice gone."

"Or people who have just never heard of Garden of Eden. That's a great idea. So you're going to enter?"

She nibbles her lower lip. "Maybe. I don't know. It's an idea."

"It's a great idea." I try to figure out why she even hesitates. Seems like a no-brainer to me. "Is there an entry fee?"

"Um, yeah, but it's not horrible. Like one-seventy-five or something."

"I'll pay it," I offer right away. Not like charity but just to take money out of the equation. If that's part of her deliberation.

She brightens, a faint smile appearing. "Thanks. You really think I should?"

"You're doing it," I say firmly. "What are your other ideas?"

"Well, this is weird, but... do you have any connections with mortuaries?"

"What for?"

"Weddings are big money, but they're also a lot of work. Casket flowers are easy money. I need to get in with some mortuaries, so they recommend me or automatically use me when they're making the arrangements."

I nod. "I'll find out. I might have a hookup. Let me see." Seems to me that every funeral I'd been to for the Family had been out of the same funeral home. I just had to ask my ma about it. "What else?"

"Weddings. I stopped at Hotel Casper, but I need to go visit all the event centers around, so they'll think of me for meetings or weddings or whatever they're hosting."

"That's good."

"The thing is, I hate that part. I like arranging flowers, but the networking part freaks me out."

I shake my head. "Nah. You got this. Like I told you when you stopped at that first hotel, you're beautiful, inside and out. Your flowers are beautiful. Everyone's gonna want to do business with you."

She searches my face like she's looking for any clue I'm blowing smoke up her ass.

"I promise, Flowers."

Our food comes, and I pick up my burger and take a big bite. It's good—better than I expected. "Any other ideas?" I prompt.

It seems I do remember how to have a conversation once I get myself into it.

Hannah's shoulders tighten. "I don't know." She uses one of those doubtful tones.

"Yeah, you do know. What is it?"

She sighs. "I was thinking about seeing if Mary Alice would renegotiate my payments. It seems to me like she'd rather get less than get nothing, right? Like if I go out of business, she's either going to have to come back here and run the place herself or lose her retirement money from me."

"That's right. She's as invested in your success as you are. She's gonna want to make this work for you."

Hannah blinks rapidly. "I really hope so."

"Text her right now and tell her you need to talk."

Hannah's eyes widen. "What?"

"Get it over with. The sooner the better. Text her now."

Hannah slowly reaches for her purse. "You sure this is a good idea?"

"Positive. Get it done."

She glances back at me a few times as she does it, like she's still not sure.

We just finish eating when her phone rings. She looks at it and flips big eyes at me. "It's her."

"Take it."

She hesitates. "No. I'll call her tomorrow." She stares at the screen. "Should I?"

"Take it," I repeat.

"Crap." Hannah swipes across her screen and puts the phone to her ear. "Hi." She stands from the table, plugging her other ear with her finger to hear. "Yeah." She looks at me and points outside then picks up her purse and hustles out the front door.

Oh fuck no. I'm not letting her stand outside on the sidewalk at night by herself. Beautiful girl like her? She's gonna get hassled.

I flag down the waitress for the check and pay it, then exit to find Hannah out front, pacing the sidewalk, her head bent like she's listening intently.

I look around, checking for anything off. Guys loitering, cars running on the curb. I don't like standing out here like I have a target on my forehead, but protecting Hannah is more important. A car drives by slowly, and I keep my eye on it until it turns the corner.

"Right. Yes. For sure. That would definitely help. It would help a lot. Thank you." She looks up at me, her eyes shining with tears. "Thank you," she chokes. "Okay. Goodnight." She ends the call.

"She said yes?" I guess.

Hannah nods with a teary laugh. "Yes. She's going to give me three months off to get back on my feet, and then I'll just pay what I can from there." She falls against me with a sob.

I slide my arms around her and burrow my fingers into her hair to massage her scalp. "That's great."

She pushes away from me. "Sorry." She wipes her eyes. "This is so embarrassing."

"No." I catch her hand and thumb a tear away for her. "I like it when you cry."

She scrunches up her forehead. "Um. That's weird." She slaps my chest. "Sick-o."

I shrug. "I don't feel. I mean, nothing at all. But you—your emotions are so big. I don't know—maybe I'll find my way back through you."

Hannah's expression goes soft and then passionate. She throws her arms around my neck and kisses me. It's one of our crazy, frantic kisses, and my dick gets hard even though I already had her at the shop.

I loop one arm around her waist and slide my hand around to roughly squeeze her ass. "Careful," I say thickly when she pulls back for air. "You're gonna get yourself fucked in the back of your van."

Her pupils are already blown, but they get even bigger, like she loves the idea. I turn her toward the van. "Not tonight." I slap her ass. "I have plans for you that involve the bed."

Chapter Nine

Hannah

I drink in the warmth of Armando's hands on my cheeks as his lips lightly graze against mine. His fingers tangle in my hair, and the smell of his cologne fills my senses. His lips are so soft, and he kisses me with a passionate fierceness that leaves me breathless.

The intensity of the kiss is building, the electricity sparking between us. We finally break apart, and I see the fire in his eyes. He looks at me with an intensity that makes my heart flutter. I could get lost in those eyes forever.

He takes my hand in his, and we make our way up the stairs to my apartment. My heart races as we enter through the front door.

"How can I thank you for everything you've done for me?" I ask between our kissing.

He breaks away with a smirk and devilish glimmer in his eyes. "Oh I can think of many ways."

Lust surges. I'm in a frenzy to unbutton his shirt and push down his pants. I need to feel his skin against me. I want to feel his mouth on mine. I can't wait another second. I need him inside me, now.

Our lips meet in an embrace of pure passion. Our tongues lock and stroke one another. His erection presses against my thigh. I have to have it inside me. I have to have him. I drop to my knees ready to please this man in whichever way he chooses.

He listens. He cares. He doesn't mind my overblown emotions.

And for that, he should be rewarded.

I pull down his pants the rest of the way, and his erection springs out, hard and thick, begging for my attention. My own body is filled with a deep need to please him, a craving that can only be satisfied by his pleasure.

I take him into my mouth, savoring the taste of him as I work him deeper and harder. His groans fill the room, spurring me on to take him to new heights of pleasure. He lets out a deep moan and burrows his fingers into my hair, gently guiding me. I use my hand to stroke what I can't take into my mouth, and I feel him lengthening and thickening in response.

A familiar wetness forms between my legs as I continue to work him. I feel him drawing near, and I move my tongue harder, deeper onto him. I can feel his pleasure mounting, can feel his muscles tightening. I want to take him to the edge, want to make him feel the way he makes me feel.

As my hand and mouth work together to bring him to the edge, he strokes my cheek, looking me in the eyes. The lust and desire in them is almost overwhelming. Pushing his pants further down his legs, I take all of him into my mouth and down my throat. I gag around the thickness, and I love the thrill from struggling to breathe. The sensual sacrifice has me doing it again, deeper this time.

"Fuck yeah," he murmurs between a moan. "Deep throat me, Flowers. Just like that."

Armando's praise spurs me to do it again and again. Each time my gagging reflex tightens around his thick cock. I continue to work him. I can feel him drawing near, and I move my tongue harder, deeper onto him.

He lets out a deep moan and tightens his grip in my hair, pulling my mouth deeper onto him. He is so close, so close that I can taste the precum. His breath catches, then he lets out a deep, rumbling moan as he comes down my throat. I swallow him down then lick him clean.

He lifts me to my feet, hands running along the curves of my body, shedding me of my clothes. Once I'm nude, he cups my breasts. Taking a nipple in his mouth, he gently teases it, sending a shockwave of pleasure through me. With hands exploring my body, feeling the curves of my waist, my hips and the wetness between my legs. I don't feel an ounce of self-consciousness when I'm with him. He clearly is turned on by every curve, every swell, and every inch of my body.

He drops to his knees and pulls me towards him. "Sit on the edge of the bed," he commands.

I oblige, and he spreads my legs and buries his face in my wetness. I throw my head back and moan as he works his tongue inside me, stroking my inner walls.

"I'm going to fuck you tonight where you've never been fucked," he warns then delves his tongue deep inside me.

I moan in response, unable to form words.

Armando continues to pleasure me with his tongue, rubbing my clit with his thumb. He pushes his tongue inside me, and the world melts away. His tongue is unrelenting, pleasure raking through me.

He spreads my legs wider, and the heat of his mouth

zeroes in on my clit. He licks and teases, igniting a burn deep in my core. The feeling builds and builds, and I find myself grinding my hips into his face.

"I want you," I gasp.

He pays no attention, keeps licking, sucking and stroking me. I grab his hair, pulling him closer, needing to feel the intensity just a little bit longer. I feel the spiral, the chain of pleasure, and I'm almost there. I'm so close I can't take it anymore.

Armando stops and looks up at me with those deep dark eyes. "I'm going to fuck you in the ass. Would you like that, Flowers?"

I nod quietly, not trusting my voice.

"Good girl."

Armando gives me a reassuring smile and guides me to the middle of the bed and lies down next to me. He leans in close and whispers in my ear, "I'm going to make you come. I'm going to make you feel so good. But you're going to have to relax. You're going to have to let me in."

"Is it going to hurt?"

"A little. But you are going to love every biting bit of it."

His lips drag across my neck, nibbling on my ear. He slides one hand down my body. I arch my back, and push my breast into his hand. He squeezes it, working my nipple between his fingers.

I feel the hardness of him against my hip, and I am overwhelmed with the desire to have him inside me—inside my ass.

He grabs me by the ankles and pulls me towards him. Spreading my legs and positioning his body between them, he places his cock at my tight back entrance.

"It's going to stretch, baby. Are you ready?"

"I'm ready," I say, taking a deep breath.

He teases my ass with the head of his penis, working it only on the outside, as if warning me of what's to come. I let out a deep breath and relax, knowing that the more I let go of any tension, the more I am going to enjoy this.

Just as he pushes the tip of himself into me, I feel the tightness and stretching. It's not bad. It actually feels good.

He begins to push into me, working his way in.

"Breathe and relax, Flowers," he whispers, as I feel him push past the tightness.

"Ow," I gasp. "It hurts."

"You're doing so good, baby. Just a little more."

Panic sets in. He may be too big for me to take this.

"Oh, it hurts," I plead.

"Just breathe, baby. Don't tense. Relax and take me."

It feels like a shock of electricity rushing through me, my body stiffens, and a shiver runs through me.

As he works himself deeper, I begin to relax. I find myself sliding into a sort of trance, feeling him slide deeper and deeper into me. He is all consuming, his flesh warming me, his cock filling a part of me that's never been touched this way before.

"Are you okay?" he asks.

I nod. "Keep going," I whisper.

Armando groans and slides deeper. He is so deep and so thick that I can't breathe. He holds himself there, deep inside me, and I feel the pleasure, the tightness begins to build inside me. It keeps growing, so full, so hot.

"You're so fucking tight," Armando moans as he pushes my legs together and strokes deeper. I feel the blood rush inside me, his length filling me.

It hurts again as he thrusts deeper. But like Armando warned—the pain feels so fucking good.

Armando begins to grind into me, sweat drops from his

body onto mine. The heat of his passion melts me, our flesh on fire for one another.

He thrusts in and out of me like a man possessed. His hands stroke my breasts. His lips are on my neck, kissing and sucking. He pulls out and works the head of his cock in circles around my tight hole. The pleasure is almost too much to bear. He guides his cock back into me, and a twinge of pain erupts in my ass. My body trembles as he thrusts into me again. Suddenly, the pleasure returns, and the pain is replaced. He pulls back and pushes in again, each time with a little more force, a little more depth. He hits my walls, over and over again—harder, faster.

I take him from every angle, the pleasure of his cock moving inside me pushes me to the brink of an orgasm. I tighten up, squeezing him. He pulls out, my ass tightening around him. He thrusts back in, and I scream in pleasure. My body erupts in fire. Each thrust is like a shockwave of carnal sensations.

He buries himself into me, as far as he can go, as deep as he can go.

"I'm close," I moan.

Armando holds his hand against my mouth, "I want to hear you. I want to hear you come for me. I want to hear you make that sweet little moaning sound."

My whole body is trembling. I push myself into him, filling myself completely with his cock. My hand reaches down, and I grab my clit, stroking it with my fingers.

"I love the way your ass feels on my cock, baby," he moans in my ear.

Armando grabs my hips, holding me onto him.

My body explodes in a mixture of orgasmic pleasure and a sharp, stinging pain. He continues to thrust in and out of me as the waves of pleasure crash over me.

I feel him explode inside of me, filling me. Each thrust pushes another wave of electricity inside of me. He thrusts once more, holding himself deep inside. He pulses and fills me, forcing me to come with him again.

Armando quickly turns me onto my side, spooning me from behind. He wraps his strong arms around my waist, pulling me closer. He kisses my shoulder and wraps his leg around mine.

"That was incredible," I say, my voice breathless.

Armando kisses my shoulder. "Are you all right?"

I nod. "I am."

"Good," he says, wiping the sweat from his brow. "Because I'm not done with you yet."

Chapter Ten

Armando

"Mando."

It's Arturo, calling me during the day while I'm at the job. Non-job. Lame place I have to go to earn a paycheck for doing nothing. I walk away from the construction area, phone at my ear. "Yeah?"

"Heard you're pissing people off down there." He chuckles.

I bristle, even though he's not wrong. Larry, the foreman, fucking hates me. I've been tailing him all week, watching what he does, asking questions. Throwing my weight around when I feel like it. Which generally comes off as questioning his decisions in front of his men. Because I don't like him and because I can.

I've been a cocksucker, but he's definitely a *stronzo*, too. None of the workers like him, and I think that's telling. But none of the workers like me either. No one wants to be my enemy; that's a given. But no one wants to be my friend either. Even the man with the doctor's appointment whom I stood up for steers clear of me. Can't say I blame any of them. It's best to avoid men like me.

"What'd you hear?" I growl.

"Don G got a call from the union guy. Asking real nice if you could work less on your no-work job." Arturo's low laugh carries across the line. "You giving 'em hell down there?"

"What the fuck else am I going to do?"

I shouldn't complain. I sound like a spoiled bitch when I have this cush job for doing jack. Trouble is, I did jack for five years. I'm sick of that shit.

"You calling to tell me to stop?"

"Nah, you do whatever the hell you want. It's your show, Mando. The don was just passing the message along. You do what you see fit with it." He pauses. "You know you don't have to even go there, right? It's all for show."

"I need to be here," is all I say.

Picking up on what I'm saying, Arturo adds, "Whatever makes you happy, man."

I should say thanks now, but I don't feel like it. I've been irritable and restless all fucking week. I got no info on who wants me dead or what they're planning next. Marco's out of the hospital, but my guilt over the incident hasn't eased. And though I'm coming to work every day, the only thing I want to do is rush home and fuck Hannah. The woman has a grip on my dick so hard that I can't explain it. I have nothing to offer her but my cock, and though she doesn't seem to mind, I have to figure out a way to give her more. She deserves so much more. But I have to force myself to leave her and come here. I have to show up and spend all day with these *stronzos*, and I keep waiting for my life to start again, but it hasn't.

It won't.

All that time in prison waiting to get out and live again, and now it's impossible. I took the prison with me.

And now I got these pussies crying to the don like the bitches they are. My mood is growing more foul by the second.

"Listen, Mando—it's my grandson's baptism on Sunday. We're having a party at my house after. I'm sorry, my daughter didn't get you an invite because she made the list before you got out. No hard feelings, eh?"

"Yeah. No. It's fine."

"So you'll be there? St. Angela's at 10 a.m.."

Fuck.

"Yeah. 'Course. I'll be there."

"Good. I'll see you then. *Ciao.*"

"*Ciao.*"

I hang up the phone, more irritable than ever. I dial Luis, who's given me jack shit since we spoke five days ago. "Yeah, what'dya got?"

"Inconclusive. What I know is that, yeah, the Hermanos have it out for you. But I suspect I'm the guy who tipped them off that you're out. Which means they didn't send the first hit, but pro'ly were the ones who blew up shit at your apartment."

I curse in Italian.

So now I have two fucking hits on my head.

Fucking great.

"I need more," I say.

"Working on it."

Chapter Eleven

Hannah

It's 6:30 pm, and he hasn't shown up. Every evening this week, Armando appeared at closing time to drive me home in the van. We ate dinner together. Had sex. Watched TV. I knew it was dangerous getting used to him being around.

I knew all along he wasn't staying. This isn't permanent.

But even so, I let myself sink into it. Enjoy the false domesticity. Cooking. Eating. Doing dishes. Him taking the trash bag or recycling box out of my hands and telling me he'd do it. Dying a little when he returned from the dumpster with empty boxes for Shadow to play in. It's obvious he has grown a fondness for my kitten, and my heart pitter-patters at the thought.

But tonight he's a no-show. I stalled. I worked late, making more arrangements than we need around here, hoping he'd show up, but he hasn't come.

My stomach tightens.

I have a phone number for him, but when I called it, there was just a generic voicemail, and he didn't answer my text. For all I know, he's changed phones by now. I'm not sure what the mafioso do. Get new burner phones every other week?

I'm not even sure that texting and calling him is appropriate. He's hiding at my house because someone's trying to kill him, and he wants to keep me safe. And we also happen to be having sex. Lots of it. But that doesn't make him my boyfriend, no matter how much it feels that way.

He already made that clear.

No matter that this deranged unlikely scenario might actually be my healthiest relationship. Because Armando sees me and doesn't flinch. And that's the most terrifying thing of all.

I get in the van and drive home, my fingers tight on the steering wheel as I navigate city traffic. It takes me forever to find a parking spot because I came home so late, but eventually, I catch someone pulling out, and I back-and-forth it thirty or forty times to fit the giant van in the small spot.

When I get up to my apartment, I hesitate outside the door.

I hear the TV.

My stomach somersaults in a weird mix of elated and pissed off. I push open the door to find Armando on my couch, feet on the coffee table, watching TV. I thunk my purse down on the table and shut the door. "You're here."

"Hey." He wears his expressionless mask that right now makes me want to kick him in the shin.

I head into the kitchen. He has boxes of Chinese takeout open on the counter, and it looks like he's already eaten.

It's one of those moments where I know I'm overreacting—I know I'm doing clingy and weird, but I can't stop the trainwreck of petty emotions coursing through me. I dump some of the food into a bowl and pick up a fork then turn around, eating standing up.

"So, I never agreed to just having a permanent roommate," I say.

He's acting casual, uncaring. It seems like a legitimate statement.

He picks up the remote and mutes the television then unfolds his large body to stand. His relaxed position on the couch was deceptive. Now he's suddenly imposing, both in size and his don't-fuck-with-me demeanor.

He walks toward me, a frown on his face.

I have to work to hold my ground and not shrink from his intensity.

"You want me to find another place to go?"

My stomach bottoms out. This is the ironic behavior of relationships—where you push away when you actually want more. I set the bowl of food on the table. Thrust my chin forward and shrug.

He gets closer, towering over me, but not touching. I *want* him to touch me—to handle me in that rough, insistent way he has, but doesn't. "Yes or no?" His tone is total authority, demanding my answer.

I swallow and shake my head, turning away.

He catches my arm and pulls me back. "What's this about?"

"Nothing," I snap, annoyed now.

"Tell me."

Maybe I don't want to be handled because I'd definitely prefer to turn away from him now. My neck and chest flush with heat. I shake my head again and look away. "I don't know."

"*Bullshit.*"

Armando has a way of saying *bullshit* that hits like a

punch. It's an assault on my senses, and I feel it everywhere. When I flinch, he pulls me even tighter, right up against his body. "Don't say you don't know when you do. Why are you pissed at me?"

I blink back the tears. Damn them! Damn him! Damn me. I'm so ridiculous!

He circles one arm around my back and brushes my curls back from my face with his free hand. "What'd I do?" he asks it softer, now.

"I'm sorry," I gulp then berate myself for apologizing. "I'm being stupid. Let's drop it."

He doesn't move, just stares down at me. "We're not dropping it. Just say it."

I shrug, defeated. It's so freaking embarrassing, but I admit it. "You could communicate a little more. You know—call to let me know you're coming here instead of the shop?"

Yep, I sound clingy. His expression turns vacant, and he releases me and steps back, just as I expected.

"I told you—I'm being stupid. You're not my boyfriend." I throw my arms in the air. "I don't know what the hell you are, but you're not that." I pick up my bowl of food again and walk around Armando, who's just standing there like a stone statue. I flop down on the sofa and turn the volume back up.

Armando doesn't move. I see nothing on the TV screen, even though my gaze steadily fixes on it. All I can do is force myself to swallow down the emotion in my throat. He's going to leave now, and that's fine. That's what needs to happen. Because the sooner I get him out of here, the sooner I can stop caring.

He walks to the door but stops and stands there, facing it. When he turns back, I dart a glance at him. "I can't be your boyfriend, Hannah." He sounds ancient. Exhausted.

I cringe. I don't want to hear this. I definitely don't want to hear this.

"I got nothing to offer. I'm fucking empty and dead and apparently one inch from having someone blow off my head."

"I know," I rush to agree, wanting to end this conversation. "Can we forget it?"

"I'm an asshole for staying here. I know I'm a dick for taking from you when I have nothing to give." He gives me a long, unfathomable look. "But I don't want to leave." He shoves his hands in his pockets.

My stomach's up in my throat, and I can't breathe. I don't know what to say.

He shrugs. "You want me to go, I'll go. That's all you gotta say. Your choice."

Like a fool, I get up and rush to him, wrapping my arms around his middle and pressing my face against his chest. His arms band around me, strong and protective. This guy would kill for me in a heartbeat. I know that already. Loyalty is his gig, and I'm under his protection.

"I don't want you to go," I admit. My belly shudders trying to hold in a sob.

He slides his hand into my curls and massages the back of my head. "Cry for me, Flowers," he murmurs, resting his chin on top of my head.

I sob a little into his shirt. "That's so wrong."

"Maybe I'll wake up," he murmurs. "Maybe I'll wake up and be your prince."

My prince. He already is my prince. Maybe that's not saying much, maybe that's just proof that I haven't dated any men of quality. Or maybe I just desperately *want* him to be my prince. I want to believe there's a happily-ever-after for the two of us. Love will conquer all and all that sap.

But for now, it's enough. Knowing he *wants* to wake up and be my prince is everything.

And I also love him for accepting my tears. Never once has this guy told me not to cry, and I've been told that my whole damn life by nearly everyone in it.

Armando tells me to cry more. To cry for him. Cry his tears.

It makes them like a tribute. Gives them meaning. Makes them pass through me more easily. I dry my cheeks with my fingers. "What are you watching?" I say to bring things back to normal.

"Old *Parks 'n Rec* episodes. Come here." He takes my hand and my bowl of food and pulls me to the couch. "What do you want to watch?"

I curl up beside him, and he puts his arm around me, tucking me into his side as he opens Netflix and scrolls through my recommendations.

"Married to the Mob," I blurt then regret it because now he's going to think I want to marry him. I'm sure my subconscious produced it because I've been mulling over the consequences of dating someone in the mafia.

"Oh Christ," he mutters but looks it up.

"We don't have to watch it," I backpedal.

"Nah, it's funny. And Michelle Pfeiffer's hot. Just don't ask me if anything's realistic."

"I won't," I promise, but I want to. I want to know everything there is to know.

Even more because he won't tell me. But I also love that he keeps the lines so clear.

Shadow mews and jumps up on the couch then promptly curls up in Armando's lap as he pulls up the movie. He sets the remote down and rubs under Shadow's chin.

"Hi, buddy," he says as Shadow starts purring loudly. "You are the coolest cat, you know that?"

I smile and join in on petting Shadow. "Sorry I was bitchy."

"Don't apologize." He kisses the top of my head like a real boyfriend. "I fucked your life up, I know." He lowers his head and brushes his lips across mine. "I appreciate you letting me stay here."

And just like that, I forgive him for everything.

Chapter Twelve

Armando

The next few days, I'm better about communicating with Hannah. I text her at the end of the day to tell her when and where I'll see her. Or what's for dinner. I was a dick that night she called me out, and I deserved a tongue-lashing. But Hannah gave me grace, and for that, I appreciate her even more.

It doesn't kill me to treat her like the queen she is. At least for now, while we're doing this. It's not a relationship because there's a deadline on it. I find out who wants me dead, get rid of them, and I can move back into my own place.

I wish I had something more to offer her, but I don't. I got nothing for anybody at this point. I'm not fit for any kind of relationship.

I stop at the mortuary on my way to Hannah's. I'd called my mom in Arizona to ask, and she gave me the name—Angel's Wings, run by a guy named Angelo. Of course he's Italian. Don G wouldn't give business elsewhere if there was a *compaesano* available. Plus, I imagine there are advantages to having a mortician in your pocket. Hiding evidence or whatever.

I push my way into the quiet lounge. There are candles burning in front of a cross and pamphlets on grieving. A thirty-something woman in a tasteful blue dress comes out to greet me. I wonder if she's related to Angelo. This doesn't seem like the kind of business you hire outsiders for. No one wants to work in a mortuary, right?

"Welcome." Her voice is hushed and respectful, like we're in a church. "How may I help you?"

"I'm here to see Angelo. Tell him it's Mando, Don Pachino's nephew."

I see recognition and curiosity glint in her eyes. Definitely a family business. She's not just some receptionist—she knows the organization.

"Of course," she says smoothly. "I'll let him know you're here."

A few moments later, a short balding man in his sixties comes out from a room down the hall, tugging the lapels of his suit jacket closed around his protruding belly. He holds out his hand like I'm an old friend. "Mando, what can I do for you?"

"Yeah. Can I go back?" I lift my chin toward his office.

He only falters for a second. He's a little nervous, but I doubt he's done anything to warrant fear of the Family. The greeting was warm, just perplexed. "Of course, come on back."

I follow him back and sit down across from his desk as he straightens a pile of papers. "I know you're the mortuary of choice for my family, so thank you for your service over the years." I'm fucking rusty at greasing wheels—real rusty. But this is for Hannah, so I'm gonna make it work.

Angelo bobs his head, still concerned. "Of course, anything for Don Pachino and his family members."

"I'll get right to the point. You order flowers for the caskets? When people don't have their own florist or don't want to do it themselves?"

"Yes." The word holds a question.

I push a stack of Hannah's cards across the desk. "I'd like you to order through this business—as a favor to me." I tap the stack. This is how deals get done in *La Famiglia*. I don't ask—I tell. But then I call it a favor.

Up to him if he wants to question whether he has to do it or if it's a polite request.

Nah, fuck that. Even polite requests get followed when you're dealing with the Pachinos.

Do I wonder if Don G would be pissed I'm throwing around his name to help the girl I'm fucking? Only a little. If he gets pissed, I'll take the heat. I didn't think it merited begging permission before I went in. I'm not killing anyone here. Just making a business deal.

Angelo picks up one of the cards and looks it over. "I'd be happy to."

There. Easy as that.

I stand up. "Appreciate it." I stand up and shake his head. "I'll show myself out. *Buona giornata*."

"*Buona giornata*," Angelo says to my back.

I don't look back.

When I get home—well, to Hannah's home, but it feels way more like mine now than that empty fucking apartment with all my old shit that I can't go back to—I find her in the shower.

I strip out of my clothes and join her for another fuckfest.

Because putting my dick in Hannah is pretty much the only thing worth living for at this point.

"Hey," she says, welcoming me to join her.

I'm not in the mood to talk. I've spoken more words today than I care to. Right now, I have one goal in mind. I flip Hannah around, placing her palms on the shower tile.

"Stick your ass out," I demand.

Hannah does as she's told, knowing that I like it when she's submissive like this.

She's so wet that my cock slides into her with ease.

The heat from the water turns us on, and we fuck with reckless abandon. She's making these little mewing noises, and her moans are loud as I ram my cock into her.

"Fuck yeah," I growl. "Just like that."

The water pelts down on our entwined bodies, her hair matted down on her face, my hands holding onto her hips tightly.

"Harder," she demands. "Give it to me harder."

I oblige her, and her moans are loud enough that they may as well be screams.

I'm slamming into her, and it's so fucking hot.

I want to come all over her ass. I slide my hand around to explore between her legs and play with her clit.

"Fuck. Oh, fuck. Oh, fuck," she cries, louder than ever.

I spank her ass as I drive deeper with each thrust.

It's animalistic. It's primal. And I fucking love it.

"Do you like when I spank you, naughty girl?"

She pushes out her ass and wiggles it. "I do."

I spank her again and again. "That's what I like to hear."

"It stings with the water," she says with a moan.

I swat her harder. "Good."

I reach around her body and spank her pussy. She squeals, and I feel her pussy tighten around my cock.

"Who's pussy is this?" I ask as I spank her pussy again.

She mewls out, "Yours. Yours."

I spank it again. "Don't ever forget it."

I push her hair from her face and lock eyes with her as I pump into her.

She's so hot.

Her face is tense. Her body is rigid from the pleasure I'm giving her.

I come deep inside of her, and she screams as she comes on my cock.

I pull out of her, and we both collapse against the shower wall.

The hot water is still beating down on us, and it feels so fucking good.

I pull away from her and smile.

"What's that look for?" she asks.

"You're mine," I tell her. At least for now. This very moment. And I'm going to enjoy every fucking minute of it.

She smiles and kisses me.

"Yeah. I'm yours."

Chapter Thirteen

Hannah

"Yes, I will be there," I promise my mom as I put together a red, white and blue horse wreath. Mary Alice had this gig every Fourth of July making wreaths for the horses in the parade downtown. What sucks is she took their fifty percent deposit before she left, so by the time I pay for the cost of the flowers, I won't make a red cent off this deal. But hopefully, they'll book again next year.

"We missed you last week," my mom complains. She's miffed I didn't come over last Sunday night for dinner. I hate obligating myself to go this Sunday—I'd rather hang with Armando, and I doubt he'd go anywhere near my parents' place, but there's no putting my mom off.

"Your dad had some medical tests done. He has high cholesterol and blood pressure," she tells me. "They're doing stress tests on his heart."

"Anything I should worry about?"

"Well, he was getting short of breath. But I got him in to

see a good specialist." My mom is a nurse at a pediatrician's office, so she knows all the best doctors in Chicago.

"Could just be because he's fifty-five and out of shape," I offer drily.

"He's not that out of shape. Your dad is still solid muscle."

"Solid muscle with a beer gut," I observe, but my mom is right. My dad works hard, and his body is in better shape than most guys his age.

"So what's new for you?" my mom prompts.

I nibble my lip, debating whether I should tell her about Armando. I hate keeping stuff from her, but what am I going to say? This mobster is hiding out at my apartment, and he can't leave because my life might also be in danger?

"Mary Alice is giving me a break on payments for a couple months, so I can get business boosted."

Thanks to Armando getting me to renegotiate.

"Are you having trouble?" My mom's voice gets tight and concerned. My parents were worried about me taking on the business. They helped me put together a down payment and wanted to help more, but my little sister, Kiana, is at SIU, and tuition is killing them.

"No, I think I'm going to be okay." I'm not sure if that's true or not, but it sure feels more true than it did a week ago. But then, everything seems easier with Armando around.

Screw it, I had to tell her. "I'm sort of dating this guy."

"You are? Bring him on Sunday!" my mom exclaims.

"Um, no, Mom. It's way too soon for that. And he's kind of anti-social at the moment."

"What do you mean, anti-social?" she asks suspiciously.

I exhale, weaving another flower through the mesh. "I don't know. He's got some PTSD going on. He says he doesn't feel anything."

"Is he military?" my mom asks.

"Not exactly. But it's kind of like that. I don't want to tell his story without his permission."

"Well," my mom says slowly. "Sounds like his brain chemistry is off. You should get him to get his neurotransmitter levels checked."

It's so obvious I wonder why I didn't put a scientific explanation to Armando's malaise. Of course it's a brain chemistry thing. Depression probably set in in prison, and the change in neurotransmitter levels wouldn't just instantly shift back because he's out. It makes perfect sense. I'm not sure he's the kind of guy I could convince to get tested or help, though.

Still, it made me feel better. It seems like Armando thinks he has some kind of fatal flaw. Soullessness. Like he's dead inside and nothing will bring him back. Maybe knowing it's just neurochemical would help him.

"Thanks, Mom, I will talk to him about it. That's a good idea."

"Well, if he wants to come Sunday, he's welcome. And we won't make a big deal about it."

"No chance, Mom. I'll see you then."

"All right, sweetheart. Love you."

"I love you, too."

I end the call as Josie breezes in late again. My stomach cinches up the way it always does when she's around these days. My beautiful best friend who's killing me as an employee. I think about Armando. What he would say. How he urged me to text Mary Alice as soon as I'd arrived at the decision. My mouth goes dry just thinking about what has to be done here.

"Josie," I start, my voice coming out like a bark.

"Yeah?" She tucks her purse behind the counter and comes over.

"Can we talk?" The flapping wings in my belly grow more wild.

I swear I see the same anxiety I feel on Josie's face.

Oh God. I don't know if I can do this.

"You know I love you, right?"

She goes still. She's wearing a bronze highlighter on the tops of her cheekbones and forehead that make her look like a model. I'm actually not sure why she isn't a model, come to think of it. She's got the beauty and the height.

"Yeah." Her voice is quiet. Almost scared.

Shit.

I'm scared too. That's why I've put off this talk for so long. I don't want to lose my best friend. I don't want to hurt or offend. But if I don't change things, I'm going to end up hating her. I think about Armando just forcing me to say why I was mad. It had been a good thing. Maybe this would be too.

"I don't know if you working here is the best thing for our friendship." I get it out all in one burst, like the air rushing out of a balloon.

Her eyes widen. "Yeah," she says, sounding sort of surprised.

I open my mouth, but nothing comes out, mainly because I'm taken aback by her *yeah*.

She runs her thumbnail over the workbench surface, eyes down. "I've been wanting to talk to you about it for a while." Her voice is low and sorry.

I blink. "You have?"

She nods. "Yeah. I just didn't want to leave you in the lurch, you know? This place is everything to you, and you're working so hard. I don't want to abandon you, but... the flower shop isn't really my gig. I want to get back to interior design, but I'm not going to put myself out there if I keep telling myself you need me."

Relief pours through me, mingled with a little hurt. "Right. You were just helping me out. Of course this isn't your gig."

"And you were helping me," she says firmly. She'd been depressed after getting laid off from her apprenticeship when I offered her the job. She was good at interior design. I figured she'd love flowers, too. We both wanted to help each other. But it makes sense that this job is holding her back from her dreams.

"So... you'll find something else?"

She nods. "If that's okay with you. I'm sorry—I've been meaning to talk to you about it for weeks, but it never seemed like the right time. My stomach's been in knots every time I was here."

"Oh my God," I let out a laugh. "That was yours!" I rub my own belly, and suddenly, now that I've identified its source, the nervous feeling is gone. "I was feeling it with you!"

Josie shakes her head. "You are so weird. Like sci-fi weird."

"I know. Star Trek—I'm Gem, the empath who steals other people's pain. Only I don't really take it out of them, I just feel it too. It's such a useless ability. Like why couldn't I be able to see ghosts or predict the future or something? Being an empath isn't a superpower, it's a handicap."

Josie pulls me in for a hug. "It's a superpower. You just haven't figured out how to use it yet. Now, what can I do to help today?"

"Casket flowers. I think Armando ordered this mortuary to give me business. The guy called and said he understood

I'd be the flower shop he'd be dealing with from now on." I open my eyes wide and cover my exaggerated "O"-shaped mouth.

"Oh my God! Married to the mob has its advantages."

"I'm not married. But um, yeah. He makes things happen, that's for sure."

Josie clucks her tongue. "I never would've put you with a guy like that, but you know what? I can see how it works."

"You can?"

She shrugs. "Yeah. I mean, aren't Italians supposed to be so passionate? And you're Ms. Emotional. So that works."

I shake my head. "He's not emotional at all. He's the opposite—like flat-liner opposite. But you're right. Maybe that's why he doesn't mind my over-emoting. He's used to it."

"Or, maybe he's just really into you." Josie waggles her eyebrows.

My fingertip touches the diamond nose ring he bought me. "It doesn't seem like it. But I don't know. I guess it's hard to tell with a guy who's flatlining on emotions."

"If you've done your crying thing and he didn't bail, he's into you. Trust me."

I give her a stupid-happy smile, wanting to believe. And also so relieved that we got work things out in the open.

I hate to jinx anything, but it seems like my life is actually starting to work. I'm facing business stuff. Friend stuff. I'm having great sex. I'm in love with a guy who accepts me for who I am and also encourages me to be something more. There are problems to be worked through, for sure. But hope is soaking in through all the broken places.

Chapter Fourteen

Armando

Hannah straddles my ass, her wet pussy sliding over my skin as her hands slide slowly up my oiled back as she gives me a massage.

It's hard as fuck to take. It isn't sex—I already thoroughly fucked her. I fucked her until the neighbors banged on the wall, and I had to yell some shit back at them to shut them up.

But this?

Almost torture. I don't like being touched.

Maybe I used to—hard to say. It's been too long to remember. I always liked being the one in charge—that's for sure. But now it's hard to take. But Hannah wants to give me this. She made a big deal about it—went and got the oil from the bathroom, looked so pleased with herself.

So I close my eyes and listen. I listen to her soft, breathy moans as she leans her weight into her thumbs, working up the ropes of my muscles. Like stroking my body turns her on. I soak in the attention she's paying to my body, the way she finds all the tight spots and works them until they soften.

And the whole time, I'm trying to figure out why she's doing this. Why she *wants* to do this.

"What did you miss most when you were in prison?" she asks. "I mean, apart from freedom?"

Oh Christ. Are we really gonna talk about prison right now?

All the work I'd done—the work she'd done—to unwind my muscles goes out the window. I feel my tone turn solid again. I'm tempted to shut her down. Just not answer or tell her I don't want to talk about it. But she's giving so much right now, it makes me feel like an asshole. So I think about the question.

"Sex would be the easy answer. I missed it most at first —before I..."

"Before you what?" she asks softly.

"Before I changed. Lost feeling. Stepped out of my body."

Hannah's hands continue to caress my back, smoothing away the ripples of discontent that come out as I speak.

"So what were you looking forward to most when you got out?"

I consider. It was mostly freedom. I didn't want to see anyone. Or anything. "Food, maybe," I admit. It's the only thing that even sounds remotely true. "My ma's baked ziti. Gio's calzones."

"You like your Italian food." I hear a smile in Hannah's voice. "All I know how to cook is spaghetti."

She says it like she wants to cook for me, which is really fucking sweet. Especially considering she's no cook, as far as I can tell. I don't even think she likes food much.

"Were those the calzones you ordered the first night you were here?"

"Yeah."

"What about the ziti? Have you had it yet?"

"No. I sent my mom out of town while things are hot for me here. I don't want her to get hurt." Now I'm talking business with Hannah—something I never should do.

But it feels right. Like she deserves these facts about me.

"Are you close to her?"

"I was before, yeah. She's the best. She'd do anything for me, you know? My dad walked out when I was eight, so it was always just me and her."

"And you got into the Outfit to help support her?" She slides her hands down my shoulders, massaging the muscles of my upper arms.

I wait a beat, knowing I shouldn't discuss any of this shit with her. "Yeah," I say finally. "Her sister is married to the don. So I was considered family, and the offer of a job was made to me. Me and Marco and Leo. They're cousins on my mother's side. We all came in together. They're like brothers to me now–as you know."

Hannah hums softly and continues kneading my muscles.

"Why are you doing this?"

"What?"

"The massage? The questions?"

She's quiet, and I figure it was a dick question, and she doesn't want to answer. Then she says, "I just want to make you feel good. That's what you do for me."

She wants to make me feel good. Not with any goal in mind beyond that. Not even an orgasm. It's not a transaction with her.

That knowledge does something to me. A fissure splits

in the metal casing around my chest. Slowly, over a period of long minutes, I let go. I let her give to me in this way she wants to.

And then I roll over and stare up at her. She stares back, her oiled hands running over my pecs, down the fronts of my shoulders. And all the while, I stare right into her warm brown eyes.

"You're beautiful," I murmur.

It's deeper than sex. Way deeper. This... this is fucking intimacy. And I must feel something. It's nothing huge. Discomfort. A soft fuzzing. A fullness in my chest.

Connection.

That's what I feel.

I'm locked on and locked into Hannah. I reach for her face and mold my hand around her cheek. I grasp her head and flip her to her back, swapping our positions. My urge is to go hot and heavy, like we always do, but I rein it in. Keep up the staring. The connection. I kiss her like it matters. Not like I'm gonna die if I don't—which is how I usually feel when I'm touching her. This time, I go lighter. I listen to the space between us. Around us. In us. My lips slide over hers, and it's sensual. Erotic but not lustful. My tongue slides in her mouth, our lips twist.

I'm hard again, and I can't stand the thought of putting on a condom. It's like I want no barriers between us in this moment.

I nudge her legs apart and push in. "I'll pull out," I promise. "I want to feel you. Is that okay?"

There's so much trust in her gaze as she nods, eyes shining like I'm her whole world right now. I glide in and out of her slowly, not working on a rhythm, just relishing every single sensation. This must be love. If I could feel it—this must be what makes people believe they're in love.

Presence.

I kiss her again, like it's our first kiss. Like I'm the kind of guy who goes slow and shows a little finesse.

Eventually we do build to a crescendo, and I'm so locked into her gaze I almost forget to pull out and come on her belly.

And that seems wrong. Like I definitely should've come inside her. I rest on my forearms and keep staring down at her until those warm brown eyes fill with tears. She stares right back, letting them leak out the sides of her eyes and fall to the pillow beneath her, not hiding or shrinking.

Giving me those tears—offering them up to me.

If only I could figure out how to use them.

But it feels like I am. Like I'm closer.

Feels like something's changing in me. Some trapped piece of humanity is finding its way out.

Every night with Hannah brings me closer.

Chapter Fifteen

Hannah

I can't help but feel cheerful as I plan the surprise date to the waterfall. My pulse skitters with anticipation, hoping the serene setting might be exactly what Armando needs to relax and open up to me. Plus, I desperately need a break from the constant grind of worrying about Garden of Eden. We both deserve this moment of respite.

"Armando." My voice trembles slightly with excitement. "I have a surprise for you."

He raises an eyebrow, his expression unreadable. "What is it?"

I step into him, my hand brushing down his rock hard abs. "If I told you, it wouldn't be a surprise."

He hesitates. "Surprises...might not be the best for me right now. Considering my situation."

I expected this kind of response. It doesn't deter me, though. I'm determined to bring some light into his life, even if it means chipping away at those walls he's built around himself.

"I understand your situation, but I promise this won't put us in danger. Here"—I toss him the keys—"You can drive." I hope giving him that measure of control will be enough to get him to come with me.

The corners of his lips tilt up slightly. "Okay, Flowers. If I'm driving." He reaches a hand out for me, and I take it as we leave the apartment and head out to the van.

He remains guarded, however, as we drive towards the unknown destination. I'm aware that the weight of his past and the dangers that still lurk in the shadows are never far from his mind. But I'm hell-bent on breaking through the wall he's built to protect himself.

"Are you going to give me any hints?" he finally asks, glancing over at me as he drives.

I'm practically bouncing in my seat, struggling to not blurt out what's coming. I've never been good at secrets. "Nope!" I giggle, shaking my head. "You'll just have to wait and see."

He lets out an almost imperceptible sigh. "Fine," he concedes, a small smile tugging at the corner of his lips. "But I'd better be impressed."

I can't contain my happiness as I notice Armando's smile. It's subtle, but it's there, and it feels like a victory. We're getting closer to the waterfall—a little hidden secret just outside Chicago's city limits, and my giddiness grows with every passing mile. I haven't been to this place in ages, and I'm questioning why as we get further and further from the city.

"Almost there." I practically bounce in my seat. "Less than thirty minutes, I promise."

Armando shakes his head, but there's amusement in his eyes. The sunshine is starting to break through his grumpy exterior. My plan may be working.

I direct him to the spot. The sound of cascading water fills the air when we finally step out of the van. The lush forest surrounding us feels like a secret world just waiting to be explored.

"Do I look like the hiking type?" he teases, but I can see he's happy.

"It's not far. Come on," I say, grabbing Armando's hand and leading him down the well-worn path towards the waterfall. "You're going to love it here."

As we walk closer to the roaring water, he scans our surroundings, taking in the vibrant greenery and the delicate wildflowers that line the trail. It feels like the perfect moment to share a piece of my past with him.

"I used to come here all the time when I was a kid," I confess, feeling a bit vulnerable as I open up to him. "It was a needed break from the loudness and the dullness of the city. This is where I first fell in love with flowers and foliage. I always knew I had to work around color and beautiful things."

"I've never been much of a nature man." He walks up and puts his arms around me. "But I am now." He kisses my jaw. "At least, I'm a huge fan of flowers."

I laugh.

"Yep, I have all the color and beautiful things I need simply by being around you."

My heart skips a beat with my victory. Armando is softening. Opening up. I can feel it in the steadiness of his embrace. I hear it in his words. And as he looks into my eyes, I see it.

He takes a deep breath. "Prison was... suffocating," he begins, his voice heavy with emotion. "Everything was gray, from the walls to the floors to the bars that kept me caged. It was hard to imagine anything else." He leans down and gives me a small peck to the lips. "Until now."

I can't even begin to comprehend what he must have gone through, but I appreciate his willingness to open up to me. I have so many questions about his time in prison, but I'll never ask. I'll simply wait for moments like this. When he willingly gives me little peeks into that time.

"I don't deserve you," he says.

"You do." I kiss him. "You're the best thing that has happened to me."

"My life..." He pauses and looks around. He motions to his surroundings. "This has never been my life. Flowers and nature and—this just wasn't my life."

"It is now." I tug him toward the final destination.

As I lead him along the riverbank, the sound of rushing water and delicate bird songs fill the air. The sun filters through the trees, casting dappled shadows on the ground beneath our feet.

As we continue our stroll, my foot slips on a particularly slick rock. Instinctively, Armando reaches out and grabs my arm to steady me, ensuring I don't lose my balance. His watchful touch sends a thrilling jolt through me, but as much as I appreciate his protectiveness, I want to show him that I'm capable of taking care of myself too. Gently, I pull my hand away from his grasp and navigate the rocks on my own.

"Everything okay?" His voice is gruff. My tough guy. Everything is a growl or a grumble.

"Everything's fine," I assure him. "I just want to prove to myself, and to you, that I can do this on my own."

He nods, seemingly understanding my need for independence, though I can see the concern in his eyes.

"Just don't bust your ass, Flowers," he says, stepping

back slightly but still watching me closely. "I've grown fond of it lately."

The sound of the waterfall grows louder as we make our way along the riverbank, its misty spray creating a refreshing coolness in the air. As we round a bend, the waterfall comes into full view, cascading down into a crystal-clear pool below.

"Wow," I breathe, struck by the beauty of the scene before us. "It's even more amazing than I remembered. It's been way too long since I've been here."

Armando takes in the serenity of the secluded spot. His gaze lingers on me for a moment, and I see the tension in his shoulders easing ever so slightly. He looks almost... relaxed.

"Close your eyes," I instruct gently, placing my hand on his chest. He hesitates but eventually complies, his eyelids fluttering shut. With my other hand, I pluck a wildflower from a nearby bush and bring it to his nose, letting him take in its delicate scent. "Smell that?" I ask softly. "That's what happiness smells like to me."

Slowly, he opens his eyes, and he leans toward my neck and inhales deeply. "This is what happiness smells like to me."

He pulls me close and captures my lips in a searing kiss. His hands tangle in my hair, anchoring me to him as we lose ourselves in each other's embrace. Scooping me into his arms, he lowers me onto a soft bed of moss near the waterfall's edge. Our lips meet again, the passion between us growing more intense by the second.

I run my hands down his chest, feeling the defined muscles ripple beneath his shirt. Armando's hands roam over my body, tracing the curves of my form. I arch my back into him, a low moan escaping my lips as he presses his body tightly against mine.

His lips leave mine, trailing soft kisses down my neck, sending shivers down my spine. His fingers hook into the waistband of my jeans, tugging them down my legs along with my panties. I moan as his fingers brush against my inner thigh, his warm breath tickling my skin.

"Hannah," I think I hear him say, over the sound of the waterfall.

He kisses his way back up my body, his lips meeting mine once again. I feel the heat emanating off his body, the bulge in his pants pressing against my thigh. I reach down to undo his pants, freeing his hardened length.

I pull him closer to me as our bodies become one. The heat between us is palpable, our desire igniting a fire that burns fiercely. I want him, need him, and he knows it. His hands travel down my body, finding the sweet spot between my legs. I gasp as he begins to stroke me, each touch sending shockwaves of pleasure through my body.

I don't think it's possible to ever tire of this man. I've never had so much sex in my life, and I'm greedy for more.

He groans as I wrap my hand around him, stroking him slowly. He kisses me deeply, his tongue tangling with mine as he positions himself at my entrance.

"I want you." His voice is gruff with desire. "I don't know if that was your intent by taking me here. But I can't resist any longer."

Slowly, he pushes himself inside of me, his hardness filling me completely. I moan loudly as he begins to thrust, each movement drawing me closer and closer to the edge. I dig my nails into his back, holding on to him as our bodies rock together.

I can feel myself getting closer to climax with each passing second. I tense my muscles and hold my breath, trying to hold back the ecstasy I know is on the horizon.

Rooted in Sin

Armando's breath is ragged, his face and neck flushed with passion. I can tell he is getting close to release, but something is holding him back.

"Come with me," I whisper in his ear, squeezing my thighs against him as I press my lips to his.

My whispered words seem to spur him on. He slams into me harder than ever, burying himself deep inside me. I cry out as I feel a wave of pleasure crash over me. My muscles spasm as I feel Armando shoot his seed into me, shaking with pleasure as he climaxes.

He collapses onto me, stealing breath from my lungs. Our bodies are slick with sweat, but we don't move. We lie together for a few moments until Armando finally pulls out of me. He kisses me slowly on the lips.

We don't speak. We only breathe.

As the sun begins to dip below the horizon, casting the world around us in hues of gold and pink, Armando and I break apart for a moment, our gazes locked. The look in his eyes tells me everything I need to know—he's in this just as deeply as I am.

Chapter Sixteen

Armando

I double park the van and throw the hazards on. We're downtown on Saturday because Hannah has to deliver a dozen horse wreaths for the Fourth of July Parade. It's a fucking zoo, which doesn't bother me. I like the energy of the city, or at least I used to, back when I felt.

Back when I wasn't looking over my shoulder every second.

Hannah's turned on by it, for sure. She's in this hot as hell white halter dress that makes her tits look edible but has me ready to slam my fist into the first guy who looks at them.

"What are you scowling about?" she asks lightly, piling a huge stack of wreaths into my waiting arms.

"Nothing," I mutter.

"Bullshit."

I look around the flowers because it's not like her to curse, and I realize she's mimicking me from the other night. She grins.

"Your fucking cleavage," I admit. "I'm gonna kill the first *stronzo* who looks at it. And then I'll have to go back to prison."

She smiles like I just told her something sweet. "No, you're not. You're going to strut your stuff because this"—she indicates her banging body with her hands—"is with *you*."

Aw, damn. I'm sort of surprised by the sensation that promise produces. Maybe I really am catching feelings because a sense of approval leaps up when she says it.

Like, *damn straight*.

I pin her with a gaze. "That"—I give her a sweeping once over—"is *mine*."

Just want to get things straight.

She arches her brows. "Oh really?"

I shake my head in warning. "Don't give me shit. I will lose it. You know how little it would take for me to bust a guy's face in."

Her smile grows wider as she pulls out the rest of the wreaths to carry herself. She likes my asshole ways.

Lucky for me, I guess.

We make our way through the gathering crowds. The parade doesn't start for another two hours, but things are already jam-packed. We find the group that ordered the wreaths and leave them with the person in charge.

"Want to stay and hang around a little bit?" Hannah's face shines bright. Her crazy curtain of curls swing down her back as she walks, sweeping her butt with each rotation of her sexy hips. She's happy today—much lighter. She and her BFF Josie had a talk last week, and Josie quit. Or Hannah fired her. But it was on good terms, and Hannah's mood lifted a ton. I should have known that relationship was weighing on her with all the other problems at the shop.

"You don't have to get back to the shop?"

She left Josie in charge today—her last day of work, but I know her friend isn't completely reliable.

"I might as well enjoy the help while I've got it," she says. "I'm going to be working on my own for a few months while I get caught up. This is my last chance to *not* work on a Saturday."

I reach for her hand and lace my fingers through hers. I swear some of her joy is seeping in. We walk through the gathering crowd, the sun warm on the top of my head and my shoulders. I stop at a Jamba Juice to buy us smoothies because it's getting too hot. Music blares from speakers on the streets, people walk by in red, white and blue clothing and face paint.

And then we pass a few guys on the sidewalk. I recognize the tattoos, but I drop my head and keep walking. After a few paces, I steal a look backward.

Fuck. Me.

They stopped and are looking back at me.

I thrust the keys to the van in Hannah's hand. "Run. Get to the van and wait for me. If I don't show in twenty minutes, drive home. Forget you knew me."

"What?" Panic flares in her eyes, but I shove her into the thick of the crowd and take off running the other way—down an alley—praying they don't try to go for Hannah to get to me.

They don't. All three of them tear down the alleyway after me.

I run hard, but my cardio abilities suck at the moment. I may have been able to keep up my physique with push ups and crunches in the pen, but we weren't exactly running laps around the prison yard.

Still, my life fucking depends on it. I'm just praising

baby Jesus they didn't have guns, or I'm pretty sure I'd already have a bullet in my back.

There's a decent chance I could take all three. Depends on if they have weapons. But we're in the middle of downtown with people everywhere, and I sure as hell don't want cops involved in this shit.

I run for the L station and manage to get in and pay before they come up the stairs. There's a security officer standing near the top, and I park my butt near him, stooping to pretend to tie my shoe.

They come up and look around, miss seeing me at first.

The train rumbles in and the doors open. I move too fast, catching their attention, and they dash over to get in the same car as me. I start running toward the end of the car, watching as they push through the throng of people to get to me. The moment the doors start to close, I leap back out.

One of them manages to get off to follow me. The other two point and shout through the window as the train speeds away.

My chest is tight from the running, and my heartbeat's out of control.

I stare at the guy who got off, and he stares back at me. It's just one guy. I could probably take him. He's not so brave without his friends. Of course, I might have to kill him like I did the hitman in the flower shop. And we're in a public place, which means I'd go down for it.

I'd go down hard.

I remember Hannah.

She's the reason I ran in the first place. To draw them away from her.

She's the reason I didn't risk it. And she's waiting for me now.

I take off, racing down the steps two at a time and jumping the last four. I just have to lose this guy and get to Hannah. I can do this, even though my lungs already feel like they want to give out.

I tear down the streets. I think the gang member is following, but I push into a crowd and lose him.

I run eight blocks until I spot the van. I look around first. No way I'm going to let anyone see me get in it if I'm still being tailed. Hannah's behind the wheel, and she starts it up as she sees me coming. It looks clear. I jump in and slam the door.

"Drive, Flowers. Fast as you can."

She nods, nostrils flared, eyes wide. Her hands grip the steering wheel in a strangle-hold.

As we tear off down the street, I catch sight of the guy.

And I'm pretty sure he sees me, too. He sees the van. He fucking sees Hannah.

"Fuck!" I explode, slamming my palm down on the dashboard.

Hannah jumps. "What?"

I shake my head. I don't want to tell her—she's already scared enough. "It's okay. I'll take care of it," I promise, even though I have no fucking clue how I'm going to do that.

All I know is no one's going to fuck with Hannah. And I'm going to make sure I stay alive to keep that promise.

Chapter Seventeen

Hannah

My heart pounds the whole trip back to the apartment. Armando makes it worse by not saying a word, yet his body is a live wire, filling the van with tension that chokes me.

It's not mine, I remind myself, remembering how the anxiety I'd felt around Josie had actually been hers. *It's not mine. It's his.*

Still, the man I care deeply about, despite my desire not to, is being hunted down like prey, so dismissing the tension is impossible.

"Who's after you, Armando? Why?" I know I shouldn't ask. He doesn't talk business, but this is the second time I have felt like I could die. I have the right to know.

He rubs his face. "I killed a guy in prison. Self defense." He shoots a dark glance at me like he's worried about my reaction to his words.

I nod. I'm actually not shocked. I knew bad stuff had happened to him there.

"He was a member of a gang. Now they're trying to kill me."

No! a voice inside my head screams. Even though I knew someone was trying to kill Armando, hearing him explain it makes me want to rage for him. He's a good guy. He has a moral compass. He follows a code. He's been mixed up in dangerous business from a young age, but it isn't his fault. He's doing the best he can with what life dealt him.

And I really want life to give him a break for a change.

I find a parking place when my mom calls. I'm going there tomorrow for dinner, so I ignore it. As soon as it stops ringing, she calls again.

I throw the van in park and pick up.

"Hannah, it's your dad," she says in a tight voice. "I had to call an ambulance for him, and I'm following now."

"What?" A sob chokes my voice. Could this day get any worse? "What happened?"

Armando goes rigid at the terror in my voice, his eyes intent on my face.

"He had a heart attack, but I kept up chest compressions until the paramedics got there. I think he'll be okay, but we'll have to see."

"What hospital?" I manage to ask.

"Cook County."

"Okay," I choke out. "I'm coming now, too."

"Thanks, baby. Call me when you get here."

"What is it?" Armando demands the moment I end the call.

"My dad." Tears spill down my cheeks. "He had a heart attack."

"Okay," Armando says softly, pushing his door open. "I'll drive, *bambi*."

Rooted in Sin

I have no idea why he called me Bambi, but I don't have the presence of mind to inquire. I tumble out of the driver's seat and let him catch me on the way down. He pulls me into a strong hug.

I soak it up—all his strength and power. His support.

We drive to the hospital in silence, me picking at a hangnail until it bleeds. Armando shooting me concerned glances. He's got someone trying to kill him, but he's more worried about me.

We find my mom in the waiting area, and I must introduce her to Armando, but it all blurs together. As we sit down to wait, I start to understand Armando's hollowness.

There's a numbness that sets in. I block out the fear, and in its place I find nothing. A total void of feeling.

I hear sounds—the television, people talking—but they mean nothing. I feel Armando's hand clasping my own but can't find any gratitude for it or even comfort.

I don't know how long we wait like that, me not breathing, barely living, waiting in the purgatory of the unknown. Of emptiness.

And then a doctor comes out. "Mrs. Munn?"

My mom surges to her feet, and Armando and I follow.

"You can come back now. Your husband suffered a mild heart attack. I'd like to keep him here under observation for the night, but he'll probably be ready to go home by tomorrow."

"Thank God," I breathe, falling into Armando. He holds me up with a strong arm around my back. His lips find the top of my head before we follow the doctor back.

As we walk in and I rush to give my dad a hug and kiss, I adjust to the shock of seeing my dad hooked up to monitors, so I don't notice that Armando's gone stiff.

"You," my dad spits, looking past me at Armando.

My mom and I gape in surprise to find him glaring at Armando.

"Why the hell are you here?"

I peer up at Armando, misgiving twisting in my gut. "You know my dad?"

"Oh no," my dad cuts in, decisively. "Not my daughter. You are not messing around with my daughter."

Armando holds his palms in the air and starts backing toward the door.

"*Armando.*" I try to stop him with my voice.

"I don't want to upset anyone." He lifts his chin toward my dad.

It's good thinking, considering my dad just had a heart attack, but I'm too upset by the fact that I don't understand what's going on.

"Wait, how do you know my dad? What's going on?"

"We work together," Armando says, and my dad snorts. Armando's at the door now. "I'll wait for you in the lobby. Take your time."

I stare at the closed door, feeling more than a little abandoned. What. The actual. Fuck? I look at my dad. "How do you know him?"

My dad frowns at me. "Tell me you are not dating that guy."

"Not exactly." I'm screwing him on the regular, but we're not officially dating. Somehow I don't think that's going to endear my dad to Armando, so I don't explain.

"He's the one you told me about?" my mom asks. "With PTSD?"

I nod, still eyeing my dad. "Tell me how you know him."

My dad tries to push himself to sit up and winces.

"Take it easy." I lay a hand on his chest. My mom slips her hand in his and squeezes.

"Hannah, honey, I hate to tell you, but that guy is mafia."

I almost laugh. "Oh. Yeah, I know, Dad. Remember I told you the building where I have Garden of Eden is owned by the mafia? I've known Armando for years."

My dad's brows drop low, and he glowers at the door. "I do not want you involved with guys like him."

I bristle, but my dad's in a hospital bed, and I probably shouldn't upset him. "He's a decent guy, Dad. But we're not officially dating, so don't worry about it."

I look at the door again. Armando didn't even try with my dad. He just backed out and left. I know he's not my boyfriend, but it still hurts. Like he didn't fight for me.

"So wait, does he work in *construction*?" I ask, hardly believing it.

"He's dead weight," my dad says. "One of those guys the mafia forces the union to give a job to. He collects a paycheck for doing nothing. He's a real upstanding guy, your boyfriend," my dad sneers.

"He's not my boyfriend." I say it firmly, like I'm willing myself to finally accept it. I mean, how much more obvious do I need him to make it? We're not entering a relationship. He's hiding out at my apartment, and we're having sex.

End of story.

I'm all hot and flushed. Now that I've seen my dad is okay, I'm itchy to get out of there. I lean over and give him a kiss on the cheek. "I'm glad it was just a small heart attack, Dad. You really scared us."

"I'm okay, baby," he tells me, catching my hand and squeezing it. "You coming over tomorrow night?"

"If you're home, I'll be there. If not, I'll come see you here. Deal?"

"Deal," he says.

"Okay, feel better, Dad."

"Be careful with that guy, Hannah," my dad warns as I reach the door. "I don't want you mixed up in the kind of trouble he'll be into."

Armando may not have fought for me, but I don't feel the same way. I turn back, defensiveness creeping up my neck. "He's not into trouble. He literally just got out of prison and is trying to figure out how to live again."

My mom's eyes go soft, my dad's mouth tightens. "Bring him to dinner tomorrow, so we can get to know him," my mom suggests, and my dad shakes his head with that resigned sort of huff.

"I don't think so," I say, my heart sinking deeper into my belly. "But thanks. I'll see you both tomorrow."

I leave the room and find Armando standing with his hands stuffed in his pockets looking sexy as hell. His face is that blank mask he always wears. I'm ready to be pissed, but then he opens his arms and folds me into them, and I let out an involuntary sob.

He combs his fingers through my curls and rubs the back of my head, and I melt into him, letting his strength sustain me.

He's not my boyfriend, but in this moment, he's enough.

He's what I need him to be.

Chapter Eighteen

Armando

We drive back to the apartment in silence. I don't have to be a mind reader to know that Hannah is upset. This is one of those times where I don't know how to do the relationship shit. Do I push her to talk? Or do I allow her to be quiet and alone with her thoughts? Finally, as we pull into the nearest parking spot, I turn off the van and reach for her hand.

"I'm sure your father is going to be just fine," I try to comfort.

"He's tough," is all she says as she stares out the window, pulling her hand free from mine.

I take a deep breath. "Have I upset you?" It's a stupid question. It's clear that I have.

She shrugs. "Not really. Maybe. I don't know." She turns her head and locks her eyes with mine. "Are you going to make me ask how you know my dad, or are you going to just offer that little bit of information?"

"We work at the same construction site," I say.

"Construction? You go to work every day in a suit." Her eyes narrow as she says the words.

"I oversee." I'm trying to give her enough information to satisfy her, but I'm uncomfortable telling her anything at all. "I helped your dad get some time off to go to an appointment with his shithead boss, and we crossed paths that way." I can see she's analyzing every word I say. "It's not like we really work side by side or anything." I don't want her thinking her dad is mixed up with the mafia or is keeping secrets from her.

Feeling I've said enough, I get out of the van, rush over to her side, and lead her upstairs hoping we can end this shitty day on a higher note. Or at the very least, we can crash and pretend it never happened.

Shadow greets us at the door, and I pick up the little fur ball, happy that someone in this room isn't sour with me. I eye Hannah as she walks straight to the kitchen where she begins doing dishes right away. This isn't Hannah. Not my Hannah.

"Okay, spill it," I say, putting Shadow down after a couple scratches behind the ear. "Tell me what I need to do to cheer you up."

"Nothing," she says, running a wine glass under the water. "It's been a long day."

"Hannah," I give my best warning voice. "I don't like games."

She turns off the water and faces me. "I don't either." There's accusation oozing from her lips.

"I don't *play* games either."

She shakes her head. "I don't even know how to explain what we are to my parents."

And there it is... something was said in that hospital room. I'd be a fool to think that nothing was. It was very obvious that Hannah's father wasn't pleased when he saw me.

"What do you want me to say?"

She crosses her arms against her chest. "Nothing, I suppose."

"Are you unhappy?" I ask, hating to think I've truly upset this woman.

"No. I'm actually happier than I can ever remember being. But I'm also... confused."

"How so?"

"One minute you are using words like 'mine' and being overly protective and possessive, and the next minute I'm realizing I know absolutely nothing about you. And then when it comes to defining us, I don't even know how to begin. And then we spend all our evenings together like we're a couple, and yet we aren't—"

My phone rings, and I think we're both grateful for the distraction.

"Go ahead," she tells me, motioning for me to pick it up.

It's Marco. "Hey," I say as I regain my composure. Hannah and I were about to go down a path that I wasn't ready for yet. I could tell she was going to start asking me questions I didn't have answers for. At least not the right ones.

"Meet me at *Sins* tonight. Leo is also coming—"

"I'm with Hannah," I interrupt, using her as my excuse to not attend the sex club that Marco loves to frequent.

"I know. Bring her. Leo and I are both bringing women as well. It can be one of those triple dates that the normal people do."

"We are far from normal," I say. "Hannah and I have had a long day—"

"Do I have to use the 'bullet in the ass' card to get you to do something with your cousin?" Marco cuts in. "Because I will. My ass will forever be scarred, and—"

"Marco wants us to go out with him and Leo tonight. They have dates," I say to Hannah.

Her eyebrow spikes, and she smiles. "That sounds like fun."

I shake my head and mouth the words 'no'.

"It would be nice to see them again," she continues, ignoring me.

"It's a sex club," I blurt out, knowing that will be enough to scare her away.

She tilts her head. "Really?"

"Stop trying to talk her out of it, dickhead," Marco chimes in from the other side of the phone. "Don't make her think it's all leather and orgies."

Hannah's smile grows. "We like sex." I can't tell if she's teasing me or not. But she genuinely doesn't seem afraid of the idea.

"My bullet ass will see you at *Sins* at nine," Marco says and hangs up before giving me an opportunity to argue any further.

"There's a sex club in Chicago?" Hannah asks.

"Several, but this one is tamer as far as sex clubs go. It's more of a high-end nightclub where there are no rules when it comes to public sex, nudity, sharing and so on."

"Will we have to have sex there?"

I choke on an unexpected laugh. "No, Flowers. We don't have to do anything."

"Will you want to?"

I pause to consider the idea. I've had sex at *Sins* before. But never with someone I considered mine. And Hannah is most definitely mine. I don't share. I don't even want anyone to look at her. I'd snap the neck of anyone at the club who even dared do a double take in her direction.

I take a step toward her and reach for her arm, tugging her against me. "What I want is sex *now*."

She looks up at me, her eyes meeting mine. A smirk spreads across her face as she runs her hands up my chest and around my neck, pulling me into a deep kiss. Our lips move in sync as she pushes me back onto the bed, straddling me.

"I'm sorry," she says. "For my... mood."

I shake my head. "Never apologize for your feelings, Flowers. I need them. I crave them."

"I don't do well with unstable," she says.

"I get it. I do."

My hands find their way to her waist, gripping her tightly as she grinds against me. I work my hands under her shirt, feeling the softness of her breasts, teasing her nipples into hard peaks. She arches her back, pressing her ass against my cock.

I give a firm squeeze, eliciting a gasp and moan from her full, pouty lips.

"I don't have the right answers to your questions. I'm not ever going to be that man. But what I can give you—" Tugging her shirt over her head, her breasts bounce with the motion, and I take a second to simply stare.

I then work a hand between her legs, rubbing her clit through her panties, drawing a moan from her. A sly grin splits her face, and she slides her panties and then her skirt off, revealing everything.

I unbuckle my belt and reach for my zipper. Hannah grabs my hands and laces her fingers with mine. Our eyes lock as she unzips my pants and tugs my belt off. She holds my belt in her teeth, and she shakes her head back and forth. I chuckle at her, and she spits it out, licking her lips seductively. She reaches for my pants, pulling them off and tossing them to the side.

Her legs wrap around me as she pulls me close, grinding against me. I slip my hand under her, but she slaps my hand away. Instead, she reaches down between us, her delicate fingers searching for my cock. Her fingertips find the head, and she rubs against it, spreading my pre-cum over her pussy lips.

I reach into the nightstand and draw out a condom. I shudder when she grabs it and slides it on, groaning at the feeling of her hand moving over me. She straddles me again, sliding down over my rock hard cock.

"So what do we do at this sex club?" she asks, her voice husky.

"Whatever we want," I say, sucking her bottom lip.

She rolls her hips, grinding against me. "What if I want to have sex for all to see?" she mouths against my mouth.

"That's fine. Just know I go back to prison afterwards," I groan, lifting my hips.

She puts her hands on my chest, pinning me to the bed as she moves up and down, taking me deep into her. I feel her nails digging into my chest, and I wrap my arms around her, holding her tight as I thrust up into her.

"Why prison?" she asks, her voice breathy.

"I'd have to kill any man who saw you naked," I answer, pushing up harder.

I speed up my thrusts, my grip so tight it's almost painful. I can feel her tightening around me, her body ready to explode.

"Then we can watch? Will that keep you out of prison?"

"We can watch, Flowers. Maybe. I might kill the man you watch, however."

"Well then maybe I'm going to just have to keep you distracted," she says as she cries out as I thrust even harder.

"I'm counting on it. Keep me out of prison, baby girl. That's your task for the night."

"Deal," she moans, convulsing around me as I erupt inside her.

Chapter Nineteen

Hannah

The city lights dance on the black car's tinted windows as we pull up to Sins, Chicago's notorious erotic nightclub, and one of Marco's favorite stomping grounds, according to Armando. He insisted on hiring a town car to take us, and it is an indulgence I'm not used to. I glance at Armando, his chiseled jawline and piercing eyes making my heart race. His tailored suit hugs his muscular frame, radiating an air of dominance and mystery that has me captivated.

"Ready?" Armando asks, his voice low and commanding. I nod, tugging at the hem of my little black dress. The plunging neckline and daring slit up the side make me feel both vulnerable and powerful, and I'm eager to see what the night has in store for us.

I would never have pegged myself as someone who would willingly enter a sex club, but I'm excited. I also love the idea that I'm getting to enter on the arm of Armando as his date. Like a couple. Like boyfriend and girlfriend.

Marco didn't just invite Armando. He invited his *woman* too.

As we approach the entrance, the pulsating beat of the music reverberates through the ground beneath us, drawing us into the seductive world that awaits inside. The velvet rope is unclipped by the imposing bouncer, and we descend down the dimly lit stairs, leaving the ordinary world behind.

The moment we enter the club, we're enveloped by its intoxicating atmosphere. The leaden lighting casts shadows on the writhing bodies around us, while the music sends vibrations echoing through my very core. My eyes are immediately drawn to the sultry performances taking place on the elaborate stage–dancers in barely-there outfits moving with hypnotic grace, their bodies entwined like serpents tempting their prey.

"Wow," I breathe, feeling Armando's hand on the small of my back as he guides me further into the club. "This place is... intense."

"Intense can be good, Hannah," he murmurs close to my ear, sending shivers down my neck.

I nod, my heart pounding in my chest as I take in the sights around me. Couples and groups indulge in various acts of pleasure, emboldened by the club's unapologetically sinful nature.

"Do I look?" I begin. "Or is it rude?" I don't know the rules. I don't want to look like the inexperienced sex club virgin I clearly am.

"Shh," he whispers, his fingers brushing against my cheek. "Don't overthink it. Just let the atmosphere guide you. You aren't going to do anything wrong."

I close my eyes for a moment, taking a deep breath and allowing myself to be carried away by the symphony of sensations that surround us. The heat of Armando's body pressed against mine, the taste of the anticipation on my lips, the sound of the music that sends shivers down my spine–all of it combines into an experience unlike anything I've ever felt before.

As we continue to explore the depths of Sins, my desire for Armando grows stronger with each passing moment. I can feel the electricity between us, our bodies drawn together like magnets as we navigate this seductive world that seems to exist solely to ignite our passion. My senses are heightened, every movement and sound feeling like an electric current running through my body.

"There they are," I say, motioning toward the VIP section where Leo, Marco, and their dates are seated. The ruby-red velvet ropes surrounding the exclusive area make it feel even more alluring.

"Ah," Armando's voice is smooth and confident, a stark contrast to the tightness in my chest as we approach the table. He leads me by the hand, his grip firm yet reassuring.

"Mando! Hannah!" Marco exclaims, his warm smile welcoming us as he rises from his seat. "Glad you could make it."

"Your *ass* didn't give me much of a choice," Armando replies, pulling me closer to him as if to remind everyone present that I am his.

"Let me introduce you to our lovely company for the night," Marco continues, gesturing to the two stunning women sitting beside him. "Isabella and Valentina."

"Nice to meet you both," I offer, doing my best to appear at ease in this unfamiliar environment. Both women appraise me with curiosity, likely wondering how someone like me ended up with a man like Armando.

"Likewise," Valentina purrs, her eyes flicking to Armando with interest before returning to me. I can't help but feel a twinge of jealousy, despite knowing it's unfounded.

"Let's get some drinks," Armando suggests, sensing the need to break the tension. "What's everyone having?"

"Champagne for Valentina and me," Isabella chimes in, batting her long, fake lashes.

"Whiskey on the rocks," Leo adds, his voice deep and commanding.

"Make it two," Marco agrees, his focus momentarily shifting from Valentina's barely-there dress.

Armando nods, glancing at me expectantly.

"Um, I'll have a glass of red wine, please," I say, feeling decidedly out of place among this group.

Armando brushes his thumb over my knuckles before turning to the waiter who has just arrived. "You heard the lady–one glass of your finest red wine, two whiskeys on the rocks, two champagnes, and for me... a scotch, neat."

The waiter scribbles down our orders before disappearing into the shadows.

"Here's to a night we won't soon forget," Leo proposes as soon as our drinks are delivered, raising his glass in anticipation.

"Cheers to that," Marco agrees, the clink of our glasses a sharp contrast to the pulsating music surrounding us. We drink deeply, the potent concoctions fueling the fire that's already burning within each of us.

As the alcohol courses through my veins, my inhibitions start to dissolve, replaced by a growing hunger for everything this night has to offer. There's so much to see. So much to feel.

"You okay?" Armando leans to my ear and asks.

I nod. "It's a lot to take in."

"Let's go for a walk. Take a look around." Armando

takes my hand and leads me through the throng of bodies, his confidence and presence commanding the space around us. As we reach an open spot, he turns to face me, his eyes locked on mine with an intensity that sends shivers down my spine.

"You want to dance?" His voice is barely audible over the pounding beat, but I nod in response, eager to lose myself in the rhythm.

"You dance?"

"No. Not at all. But I will for you."

My chest warms. This guy. I'm addicted.

As the music swells, Armando and I move closer together, our bodies instinctively finding their own beat within the chaos. Our hips sway in sync as we dance, his strong hands guiding my movements with electric precision. The heat between us grows with every passing moment, and I'm lost in the delicious friction it creates.

"I'm never going to hear the end of this from Marco and Leo." Armando leans in close, shouting into my ear so I can hear him. "I feel like a brick wall gyrating."

I laugh loudly, appreciating that he's giving me something to help put me at ease even if it means he's out of his element. Armando may not be able to give me the right words all the time, but he certainly knows how to give me the right actions.

My body moves with newfound fluidity, uninhibited by doubt or restraint. Armando's gaze never leaves me, and I feel a surge of pleasure knowing that I am the sole object of his attention.

I become increasingly aware of the illicit activities taking place around us. Couples entwined in various sex acts, some concealed in shadowy corners while others brazenly display their passion for all to see. Kinky play unfolds before my eyes, a world I had only ever glimpsed in whispered conversations and late-night fantasies.

The sight of these unapologetic displays of desire only serves to fuel the fire growing within me. I feel a primal urge to explore this darker side of my own sexuality.

"Armando," I breathe, my voice barely audible above the music as I glance around at the debauchery surrounding us. "This is... no words to describe it."

"Is this place too much?" he asks, his dark eyes searching mine for any sign of discomfort.

"No," I reply, surprising even myself with the conviction in my voice. "I'm intrigued."

"Good," he grins, pulling me closer until our bodies are flush against one another.

The pulsating beat of the music seems to vibrate through my bones as Armando and I dance. The heat between us is palpable; the air around us crackles with electricity as we share heated glances and stolen touches.

"Your heart's racing," Armando murmurs huskily into my ear, his breath hot against my skin, sending shivers down my spine. "Is it the excitement, or is it me?"

"Maybe a little of both," I admit, feeling bold under the euphoria of the night. Our eyes lock, and for a moment, everything else fades away—the music, the people, our friends. It's just us, and the undeniable connection that's been growing stronger since the moment we met.

He watches me intently, his gaze dark and possessive, feeding the fire within me. I can feel his need for control, his desire to protect me, even in this chaotic world we've chosen to explore together.

As we dance, I catch sight of Marco and Leo at the edge of the dance floor, their laughter mingling with the music. Their dates have moved closer, body language open and inviting, as they engage in flirtatious banter. Leo brushes a strand of hair behind his date's ear, his smile all charm and mischief, while Marco leans in to whisper something that makes his date giggle and blush.

Every now and then, they glance over at Armando and me, their approving smiles telling me that they're happy to see us together.

I place my hand on his chest as the music continues to pound around us. "Let's take a break from dancing and explore more of Sins. I'm curious to see what else this place has to offer."

"Are you sure?" he asks, his dark eyes searching mine for any sign of hesitation.

"Absolutely," I reply with a smile, feeling a thrill race through me at the thought of venturing deeper into this mysterious world. "I want to experience everything tonight."

"Just don't put me back in prison," Armando says, his lips curving into a dangerous smirk as he takes my hand.

As we weave our way through the heated crowd, I notice how other patrons are drawn to Armando—both men and women alike. He exudes a raw power that is impossible to ignore, and I feel a surge of pride knowing that he's mine for the night.

We discover hidden rooms and secret corners where couples and groups engage in even more sinful activities than those taking place on the main floor. The scent of sweat and arousal fills the air, along with the low hum of moans and whispers carrying the secrets of the night.

"Look at them," I murmur into his ear, as I nod towards a couple entwined together on a velvet chaise lounge. "They're lost in their passion, completely unaware of the world around them."

"That's how I feel with you," Armando confesses. "Everything else is blocked out."

My heart pounds in my chest as I turn to face him. I pull him into one of the secluded alcoves that line the perimeter of the club. It's dimly lit and hidden from view, offering us a moment of privacy amidst the chaos.

He kisses me deeply, his hands slipping around my waist as he pulls me closer.

My fingers trail up his chest to cradle his jaw. His gaze never leaves mine as we stand on the precipice of surrender.

"I'd fuck you here," I whisper, closing the distance between us as our lips meet in a searing, passionate kiss. "But I want to keep you locked up with me. Nowhere else."

Our mouths move together, tongues exploring and tasting each other, as the heat between us grows more intense with each passing second. Armando grips my hips tightly, pulling me flush against him, so I feel his arousal pressing against my thigh.

"I can't share you, Flowers. At least not yet. I'm a greedy bastard that wants that hot piece of ass of yours to myself," he says, his voice rough with desire as he rests his forehead against mine. "But I promise that when I get you home, I'm going to have you screaming out my name."

"Promise?"

"Fucking count on it," he replies, his eyes dark and full of promise.

We emerge from the shadows, our hearts still racing from our passionate exchange, and make our way back to the VIP table. As we approach, I see Leo regaling everyone with a story, his hands animated as he narrates some wild experience. Marco, sitting beside him, nods along in agreement while their dates listen with rapt attention.

"Ah, there you two are!" Leo exclaims, spotting us. "We

were just discussing the unique... entertainment Sins has to offer."

"Unique is certainly one word for it," Armando agrees, a wry smile playing on his lips as he pulls out a chair for me. I slide into the seat, feeling the buzz of excitement and anticipation still coursing through my veins.

As the conversation continues, laughter and teasing filling the air, I can't help but steal glances at Armando. The connection between us has only grown stronger tonight, and I can feel the heat of his gaze on me, even when I'm not looking directly at him. His strong hand rests on my thigh, a silent promise of what's to come.

But also a certain kind of... possession.

He's used the word 'mine' multiple times. Always in the heat of passion. But right now, sitting and laughing with his cousins, I actually feel like his. Truly his. And I love it.

Time seems to slip away as we share stories and jokes, each of us lost in the thrill of the night. But eventually, even the most magical of moments must come to an end.

"Looks like they're starting to close up," Leo observes, noting the staff beginning to clean up around the club.

"Guess it's time to call it a night," Marco agrees, standing and stretching his arms overhead.

"All right, let's get out of here," Armando says, rising from his seat and extending a hand to me.

"Goodnight, everyone." I wave to our friends as we make our way towards the exit.

"Good job getting Mando out of the house," Leo says to me. "You're good for him."

"She's a keeper," Marco adds, filling me with pride. Nothing is a better feeling than winning over the family of the man you... love.

Stepping out into the cool night air, the muffled sounds

of *Sins* fading behind us, I squeeze Armando's hand, eager for whatever comes next.

"Tonight was fun," I say.

"It's just beginning. I made a promise to you, remember?" Armando says, his voice low and full of promise.

Chapter Twenty

Hannah

"What if I had insisted we have sex at Sins?" I ask as I strip down naked before Armando, not giving him any doubt what I have in mind for the remainder of the night. Seeing all those naked bodies ignited something inside me. Something darker. More primal.

"I would have fucked you," Armando answers, also removing his clothing. "But not like I plan on fucking you now."

I raise an eyebrow. "Oh yeah, and how is that?"

"Harder than you've ever been fucked before."

My heart double-pumps. My knees get weak. But I'm definitely having whatever he's offering. "I'm not afraid," I tell him, with a note of challenge. "I've taken it hard before."

"Yeah?" He saunters toward me, his eyes dark with intent. "Prove it." He sprawls onto the bed completely naked.

I smile and step up on the bed and crawl toward him, never taking my gaze from his. I circle my arms around his body. Deeply. Passionately. Wantonly.

He wraps me in his arms and flips me to my back, his tongue dancing with mine. He tastes like scotch, and it's a good scotch, I can tell. I like the way it tastes on his tongue and the way he tastes on mine.

"Tell me what you want." He lifts my chin, forcing me to look into his eyes.

"I want it... kinky. Dark. I want to feel... submissive to you," I confess, feeling safe to admit my darkest desires. "I don't want gentle. I don't want caresses. I want it dirty. The way you like to give it."

I don't know what got into me and why the request is coming so easily. But we just left Sins, and if there is ever a time to completely let go, now is it.

"You want me to fuck you hard?" he pushes. "Push you around a little? Fuck you like the dirty little slut you just admitted you want to be?"

"Yes," I whisper.

"I'm going to do all that to you and more." His smirk is dangerous.

"Don't hold back," I breathe.

"Roll over, I want to see your ass," he orders, releasing me and climbing off.

"Like this?" I roll to my belly.

"Up on your knees, Flowers."

I step up on my knees and bend over, then look over my shoulder at him.

"Exactly like that. Now spread your cheeks."

I do as I'm told, and he strokes his hand over my ass. I hear the snap of the tube of lubricant and his slickened fingers slide over my pussy, his thumb at my asshole. I shamelessly push back onto his fingers, begging for more.

"You want this?" He slaps my ass hard with his other hand, then rubs the hurt away.

"Yes. I want you to fuck my ass."

"What else, Flowers?"

"I want you to get rough with me. Fuck me so I can't walk straight. Until I can't even think anymore. All night long."

Armando growls and plunges his fingers inside my pussy.

"I want you to slap my ass until it's red and sore."

"Fuck, baby. You're getting me harder than stone. What else am I going to do to you?"

"I want you to..." I almost don't dare ask for this one. But it's a fantasy I've had since the day he showed up in my flower shop.

"What, Flowers?"

"Choke me."

"Yeah? I'll choke you, baby. You want a hand necklace while I fuck you hard?"

"Yes, please."

"You like a little fear with your sex? Want me to cut off your air? Or just pretend, baby?"

I grow dizzy, scarcely believing we're having this conversation. That my fantasy is actually going to come true. "I want you to cut off my air... make me feel like you're about to end me. Like I'm about to die for you."

The room spins. I'm terrified by my request, but I go on. "I want you to own me. Make me yours and only yours. Your slut. Your dirty girl. Yours."

I've never said any of these words aloud before. Never thought them. But Armando awakened something in me. He's shown me I can trust him with my body, even when there's a little violence involved. And after all the crazy things we saw tonight, it feels safe to ask for this. As I speak, I realize that's exactly what I'm doing. I'm letting him in, and more importantly, I'm letting myself out. I'm freeing myself from a lot of my fears and insecurities, and I'm hanging on to Armando's every word, waiting for him to tell me what to do next.

"That's so hot, Hannah. You are my dirty girl. I'm gonna give it to you good, Flowers."

He keeps working his fingers between my legs, sliding his thumb into my ass, all the while peppering my cheeks with slaps. A chaotic, exotic mix of stimulation that heightens everything I feel. I moan. I'm drowning in lust. So far beyond my normal inhibitions.

Mando puts a pillow beneath my hips and pushes me down over it then climbs between my legs. He rubs the head of his cock over my pussy as he grips my hair, twisting my head back, so I'm forced to look up at him.

"I'm the only one that's going to fuck this pussy," he commands at the same moment he pushes inside me.

"Oh God." My internal muscles squeeze around his cock. I'm already orgasming from just one stroke.

He goes slowly, arcing in, sliding out, teasing me. Torturing me.

"Spank me," I plead, wanting more intensity.

"Spank you?" He pulls out of me. "You need to earn that spanking."

"How?"

"Beg me for it." He slaps my ass a few times, and the pain is sharp and intense, but I love it.

"Please," I plead, needing to feel that heat radiating from my ass and spreading throughout my whole body. "Please, Armando. Please spank me harder. Please."

He does it again and again, until my ass is burning and stinging. It's exactly what I crave. What I need.

"Good girl." He pulls me around to sit me down on the edge of the bed. "Now spread your legs for me."

I do as he commands, and he gets on his knees in front of me, gripping my thighs and spreading them wide.

"Look at you," he says. "Your pussy is so fucking wet, and your pussy lips are swollen."

"Your cock made me that way," I say, reaching out and gripping his cock, stroking it hard.

"Show me how much you want my cock," he says, taking his cock and rubbing it up and down my pussy. "Suck my cock and show me how much you want it. I want you to taste how much your pussy loves this cock."

I watch his cock enter my mouth, and I swirl my tongue around it and lick it, paying extra attention to the head and the sensitive area underneath his cockhead.

"That's a good girl," he encourages while gripping my head and pushing his cock deeper into my mouth. "Take it all."

I do, and as I suck on his cock, I feel him take one of my hands and wrap it around the base of his cock, and he guides my hand up and down his cock while he fucks my mouth. I'm moaning so hard, I'm sure that my neighbors can hear me, but I don't care. I've never felt so free and so wild.

I want this every night. I want to be his dirty little whore. I want him to make me feel beautiful and wanted, opening my mouth wide and lifting my chin up so he can fuck my face however he wants.

I want everything he is willing to give me.

I want to be possessed by him.

He fucks my face harder, and I struggle to take it, but I take it. I take it all. I look into his eyes and see the intensity and the passion. I see his desire, and it's a beautiful thing.

I'm his beautiful, dirty girl, and I love it.

I love him.

"Make me come all over my dirty girl's face," he commands, and I pull my mouth off his cock, stroking it hard and fast. He starts to breathe hard, and I know he's close.

"Do it. Come all over my face."

He comes hard. Ribbons of his cum hit my face and splash against my cheeks, and I rub it in immediately, letting it drip down my face as I make sure to get it in my mouth.

"That's a good girl." He wipes away the cum from my face with a nearby towel. "Now get on the bed and wait for me."

I do as I'm told, and as I lie on the bed and look up at him, I'm in awe of what he is.

"Time for your spanking. You earned it. Roll over, ass in the air."

I do as I'm told, and I feel my body shaking with excitement.

"Spread your legs," he says, rubbing my ass with his hands.

I spread my legs, knowing that I belong to him and that he is slowly taking over my life.

And I'm fine with that.

I'm fine with being his dirty little whore forever.

He slaps my ass a few times, and then he lifts it up and squeezes it. He spanks my cheeks again, and I feel the sting in my ass, and it makes my pussy tingle even more. He spanks me until my ass is red and stinging and burning. It hurts, but it feels so good at the same time.

"Spread your ass apart," he commands. "I want to see all of that beautiful pussy."

I spread my ass apart and look back, eager to see what he's going to do to me.

He slaps my ass, and then he takes my hand and places it between my thighs, rubbing my pussy.

He slaps my pussy with my hand, and then he slaps my pussy again, and then he puts my fingers in my mouth and forces me to suck them.

"You're a dirty girl," he says. "Taste how dirty you are."

"I'm your dirty girl," I agree.

"And I'm your Daddy," he says, spanking me over and over, making me cry out loudly. "I'm the one who fucks this pussy, this beautiful pussy."

"Yes, Daddy," I agree, crying out in passion as he hits my pussy harder and harder.

"And this ass belongs to me," he says, slapping my ass so hard I feel the pain radiating and spreading.

"It belongs to you. Only you."

"That's right," he says. "Only me. You're mine."

"I'm all yours."

"Good girl." He slaps my ass again.

"And now I'm going to make you come with my tongue," he says, spreading my ass cheeks with his hands. He puts his tongue in my ass, and I moan loudly.

"My dirty girl likes that," he says. "You like when I rim this asshole of yours."

"I like it a lot," I agree, my pussy dripping wet.

He licks my ass, and I can't help but grind against his face.

"I'm going to make you come like you've never come before." He rubs my pussy and then slides his fingers inside me and pumps hard.

I start moaning, and it doesn't take long before my body is shaking.

"Come on my fingers, baby. Come all over them."

His words are dirty, and they're nasty, and they're exactly what I want to hear.

"Come for me, Flowers," he says, and I do, my body shaking and shuddering and convulsing.

He holds me close to him as my body comes down from the rawest, dirtiest orgasm ever.

We lie in the darkness together, our breath mingling. Our heartbeats slowing from a gallop.

"Thank you," I murmur softly.

Armando lets out a chuff. "You're thanking me? No, baby. You're fucking amazing, Hannah."

His words make my heart sing.

And that's the real danger. Not how this man handles my body.

But how he handles my heart.

God I hope he doesn't crush it.

What's even scarier is that he has the power to break my soul.

Chapter Twenty-One

rmando

I'm running through the streets of Chicago, being chased by the Hermanos. I get knocked down and cornered by the entire gang, all of them pointing pistols at me. But then the faces turn familiar—one of the guys in my face is Emilio, another is Harold, Hannah's dad.

I climb to my feet and offer my chest as target. "Do it," I say, but then I hear Hannah calling my name.

Armando.

Hearing her voice changes my plan. I can't let her see me die. I can't die when she might need me. I decide to try to fight my way out of it or to escape. I grab the wrist of the nearest guy to wrest his gun away.

"Armando!"

I gasp, sitting bolt upright in the bed, my fingers closed around Hannah's wrist in a crushing grasp.

"Oh, shit!" I drop her wrist like it's on fire then snatch it back up again, gently. I kiss her racing pulse. Her eyes are wide and horrified.

"I'm sorry, Flowers. I'm so sorry." I press her wrist to my lips again. "I hurt you. Fuck."

She's naked, her beautiful brown breasts shifting as she adjusts to sit up as well. "It's okay," she whispers, looping her arms around my neck in a strangling hug.

I don't deserve her forgiveness, and I suspect there's sympathy mixed in there, too, which makes me itchy and angry, but I can't reject her sweetness. She's the fucking reason I want to live if I analyze the damn nightmare.

Our sex we just had before we passed out was... fucking animalistic, and I now worry. Am I being too hard on her? Am I allowing the darker side to come out of me too quickly?

Fuck. Am I fucking this up? I called her a whore. A whore!

Hannah deserves better. She deserves a man who can give her flowers and candy and whisper sweet nothings. I'm not this man.

"Let me make you feel good," I beg because sex is pretty much the only thing I have to offer these days, and she fell asleep in the middle of last night.

She lets me push her to her back and crawl down between her legs, satisfying her with my tongue before I let myself sink my cock into her.

We finish and I roll out of bed and into the shower. It's Arturo's grandson's baptism, so I have to put on a suit and go to mass this morning.

When I come out, Hannah heads into the shower, and I get dressed and make us coffee.

I hand her a mug when she comes out with a towel wrapped around her luscious curves.

She sets it down without drinking any. "Thanks but my stomach's off this morning. Where are you going?" she asks. It kills me that she looks like she doesn't expect me to answer. Or like she doesn't deserve to ask. It kills me that I don't have more to give to Hannah Munn, the girl who offered up her whole world to me when I didn't ask nicely. When I didn't ask at all.

"A baptism. And the party afterward."

I see hurt flicker over her face and feel the knife in my chest twist deeper. I want to invite her. Hell, nothing would make me happier than having Hannah at my side. It would make dealing with Emilio and Grace so much easier, it would stop all the stares and whispers of everyone wondering how I'm dealing with Emilio and Grace.

"I'm going to my parents for dinner. You're, um, welcome to come," she says, but her normal morning glee is void from her tone.

Fuck. I rub my shaved jaw. "I don't think that's a good idea, Curls. Your dad didn't exactly love the idea of me hanging around you."

Of all the men in the world, Hannah's dad had to be on the same job site as me. At least I have the very small satisfaction of having backed him up when he asked for the doctor visit.

Fuck, probably the doctor visit that should have prevented this heart attack.

"You working today?" I ask.

"Yeah."

"'Kay. I'll go there after the party. See if I can help you with anything."

She nods, but I still see the hurt in her face. I brush my lips across hers. "Be good, Flowers. I'll see you soon."

* * *

The baptism party is like any Family party. I've been to a thousand of them, but this one is excruciating. Almost as painful as my welcome home party.

Marco and Leo stick near me, and I do my best to not look like a sullen cunt although I probably don't succeed.

Fucking Grace has to come over again—I swear she must be suffering from more guilt than I gave her credit for. But then, there was a time when I thought we truly loved each other. Just because my heart is darker than night now doesn't mean she doesn't still feel the pull of what we once had.

She just doesn't know that guy is dead.

"Hi Mando," she says, all breathless. "Listen, um, this is awkward." She shoots a glance at Marco and Leo, who hold their ground.

I don't tell them to do anything different.

"I just wanted to say, um, that I have your invite to the wedding. I just—I couldn't decide which was worse—to send it or not to send it." Her eyes swim with real tears, which takes me by surprise.

"Aw, Grace." I'm suddenly so fucking tired. Too tired to deal with any of this shit. What does she want me to say? That she's forgiven?

Eh. Maybe she is. I don't know.

Seeing her standing in front of me right now with her perfect makeup and her fake nails, it just brings home how superficial our relationship was. We were together because we looked good together. We fit, in terms of the Outfit and the circles we ran in. She wanted a guy who flashed the money around. Who treated her nice and fucked her good. Who played all the romantic gestures right out of the playbook.

I did that for her. She did what she was supposed to do for me—look pretty on my arm. Say the right things at Family gatherings, do what she was told.

It wasn't a relationship. It was two people playing at one. We did it well. Until we didn't. Because prison didn't fit the role she wanted from me.

Hannah wouldn't write me off when things went wrong. Hell, everything with Hannah has already gone wrong. I've killed a man on the floor of her shop. Tied her up and held her prisoner. Offered her nothing of my dark, dead heart.

And still she cries for me. Still she wrapped those arms around my neck when I had a bad dream, even when I nearly broke her wrist for trying to wake me.

I love her.

The thought hits me like a bowling ball. Especially because I don't know what to do with it. I can't be what Hannah deserves.

If I had any kind of decency, I'd move out and leave her out of my mess right now.

I stare at Grace, my gut churning. "Yeah, Grace, I'd rather not come, honestly. But thanks for asking. Listen, I have a question, though."

"Yes?" She raises her manicured brows.

"You order your flowers already?"

Confusion flits over her face. "Um, no, but I'll be doing it this week, why?"

"Make sure you get them from Garden of Eden. They're award-winning. They do all the best weddings." It's the old Mando talking. The one who cared about designer names and having the best of everything. Because I know Grace still cares about all that shit.

Her eyes widen. "Oh, okay. Is that the place you used when you sent me all those—" she breaks off and swallows.

"Yeah," I say softly. "They did a great job, right? They're even better now. Like best in town."

I notice Marco and Leo looking at me speculatively, but I ignore it.

If I can get Hannah some business out of Grace and Emilio's fucking wedding, I'm going to do it.

"Okay, I'll call them tomorrow. Thanks for the tip." She looks at me again, regret soft on her face.

I'm a bastard because I still don't feel like letting her off the hook. But when she turns away with slumped shoulders, I say her name, softly.

"Grace."

She turns back.

"Thanks for checking in with me," I say. It's the best I can offer her at the moment, but it seems to be what she needs. Relief floods her face and she nods, smiling sadly.

"Of course. Good luck, Mando. With everything."

"Yeah, you too."

I watch her walk away, and Marco waits until she's out of earshot to say, "She's still a cunt."

I've forgotten how to smile, but the corners of my mouth twitch. "Yeah, she is," I say, but there's nothing behind it. And not the dead, blank nothing I felt when I got out, but really nothing. An empty space, waiting to be filled.

Maybe I really am coming back to the living.

Chapter Twenty-Two

Hannah

A week of feeling seasick.

Not being able to drink the wine Armando pours for me with dinner. I'd be stupid if I didn't consider the possibility.

We've been careful... sometimes, even most of the time. But fuck... not all the time.

I remember the odds from high school health class. They're not great.

I pick up a pregnancy test on my way home, rushing to get there before Armando does.

The queasiness in my belly grows, probably from nerves, and by the time I get home to my bathroom, I'm doubling over it and retching.

Ugh.

This shouldn't be happening.

I'm with a guy who doesn't even want to be my boyfriend. Being with Armando is like being on a roller-coaster of emotions. But this could throw us off the tracks, plunging toward the hard reality down below. An unplanned pregnancy is not going to help matters.

Or maybe it will, my stupid little voice of hope whispers.

No, it won't. I try to savage it with bared teeth.

Shadow meows and threads his soft little body around my ankles, purring. I ignore him and read the directions for the test. I should wait for my morning pee, when the hormones would be the strongest, but I'm too wound up. I've bought the damn thing, and I need to do it now. I sit on the toilet and aim the stick in my stream of pee. Then sit there and wait.

My belly flutters out of control when the results appear. A faint positive line.

Tears spear my eyes, but I'm not devastated.

Strangely, it's a mixture of excitement and fear that churn together.

And, of course, before I even have time to get my head on straight, I hear Armando walk into the apartment.

Shit! I don't know what makes me throw the test into the kitty litter box and cinch the bag up for the trash, but I do. I rush out of the bathroom, somewhat desperate to get rid of the evidence before he sees it.

"You want me to take that out?" He reaches for the knotted bag of dirty litter.

"*No*, I'll take it out." Dammit, I sound breathless. My strange behavior doesn't go unnoticed. Armando's eyes narrow, and he cocks his head.

"Be right back," I call as I sweep out the door.

Nausea hits me hard on the trip downstairs. I gag at the dumpster, the nasty smell pushing me over the edge. I run away from it, my belly heaving, but fortunately not pushing the contents of my stomach all the way up and out.

Ugh.

When I get upstairs, I find Armando in the kitchen holding the cardboard box the test came in, a stunned, unhappy expression on his face. "Fuck, Hannah."

It's hard to believe in the course of two minutes a mama bear energy could enter me and take hold, but it does. I'm instantly on the defensive, and protecting my baby is all that matters.

"Fuck!" he says louder, turning to face the wall and punching it. His knuckles break through my drywall, sending crumbles to the floor. "It's my fault. I didn't use a condom all the time. I let our passion take over, and... fuck!"

And with that, he finally crushes my hopeful pink Cinderella heart. There will be no happy ending for us. He's not a prince. He's not even a boyfriend.

He doesn't want me or this baby. And I'll be damned if I'll let him taint any part of this pregnancy. And suddenly, things become crystal clear. I have a tiny life growing inside me that I need to protect. Honor. I need to do for my baby what I couldn't do for myself.

Demand more.

Demand *a lot* more.

And Armando is not going to give that to me. He simply can't. He's made that abundantly clear.

"It was negative," I say loudly, suddenly grateful for my instinct to bury that evidence with the kitty litter. "I'm late, but I'm not pregnant. I just wanted to be sure."

Armando swivels back slowly and eyes me.

I'm not the best liar, so I hide it under bluster. "But this pregnancy scare brought it all home to me." I suck in a ragged breath. "It's time for you to leave, Armando. Things are getting too complicated." My eyes fill with tears, and for once, I'm not ashamed. They're honest tears and only serve to strengthen my resolve right now. "I don't want a broken heart. It's already cracking. I'm cracking. I can't do this anymore."

The color drains from Armando's face. I might've celebrated the fact that he had an emotional reaction to anything under different circumstances. But as it is, his shock and pain reverberate through me, shattering what little control I have left.

"You want me to leave?"

I nod.

"But I need to keep you safe."

"You can do that from afar. Keep your men on me," I suggest. "You and I both know you being around me is putting me in more danger than you staying. And you staying here—"

"Hannah..."

I start to cry in earnest. I'm sure the hormones aren't helping. "I need you to leave," I say through my tears.

Armando's eyes go dead. He launches into action, his movements jerky and mechanical. He moves through the apartment and packs his things into the duffel bag he brought over. He picks Shadow up from the floor where he's twining around his ankles. He brings him up to his face and kisses my kitten's head. "Take care of her, you hear me?"

He walks to the door. "I'm sorry, Hannah." His voice is tight and gruff.

I nod, closing my throat around my sobs.

It feels so wrong, but I know it's the right thing to do. I'm not saddling this baby with a father who doesn't want him. I'm not going to have the discussion with Armando about whether or not to keep it.

I'm keeping it. And he's got to go. That's all there is to it.

I don't have room in my life for a non-boyfriend. Not when this baby's going to need everything I have to give it.

He looks at me like he wants to say something else but then just nods and turns back to the door. He opens it, walks through and closes it without looking back.

And the moment he's gone, I drop to my knees and sob.

Chapter Twenty-Three

Armando

The world dims the moment Hannah tells me to leave.

I know it's for the best. I've known all along I should leave because I'm fucking toxic to her. I have zero to offer, and on top of that, every minute I spend with her puts her life in danger with the people who want me dead.

And Christ, when I thought she was pregnant, I couldn't think of anything worse. Endangering a helpless infant? I'd have to leave her—never see her again, not even as a friend.

So her making the decision for me should've made it easier.

It should have.

But a grey haze descends around my vision as I stand out on the street with my duffel bag and try to figure out what the fuck I'm going to do.

And then, because I honestly didn't give a fuck if the Hermanos want to kill me now, I head to my apartment.

I take the L because I can't stand the thought of being cooped up with an Uber driver. At the apartment, I pass the landlord in the hallway, and he gives me the stink eye.

I can't even bring myself to react. Not a look. Not a blink. Definitely not a grunt of hello.

Go fuck yourself is what I say in my head.

And then I find myself pounding on Marco's door. Not because I need a shoulder to cry on. Fuck that. But because I'd love somebody's face to pound, and chances are good Marco's got someone he needs to send a message to—from the don.

"Hey, what's up?" Marco asks, pulling the door wide and studying my face.

I don't say anything, just stalk in without seeing him or his place.

"You got anybody to send a message to?"

Marco gives me a wary look. "You need to put the hurt on someone?"

"Yeah."

Marco shoves his hands in his pockets and angles his body half away from mine, like he doesn't want to bear the full weight of my focus if it's directed at him. "Hannah?"

Some of the blur in my vision clears at having my problem named.

"I don't want to talk about her," I snarl because, like I said, I'm out for blood right now.

"You guys seemed super tight the other night. You've been inseparable. What happened?"

In a flash, I slam his back against a wall, my forearm choking off his windpipe. "Stop asking me about her."

I think he hisses something like *cocksucker* through his bared teeth.

"It's over, and you're never going to speak her name again."

He pinches his lips and grinds his teeth together while I continue to cut off his air flow. Finally he punches me in the ribs. Twice.

Hard.

I loosen my grip on the second punch because it knocks the wind out of me.

"Peace, Mando." Marco's hands are in the air when I lift my head. "Chill, man."

I want to punch his teeth out so badly, but I also love him too much to do it.

"What the fuck's going on?" Leo appears in the living room.

Marco side steps, keeping his shoulders squared to me like a boxer circling his opponent. "Mando wants to kill someone. I'm trying to keep that guy from being me."

Aw, fuck it. I take a swing at him. He ducks and plows into me, knocking me onto my back. In a moment, both he and Leo are sitting on me, holding me down.

"Girl problems," Marco says to Leo.

"Fuck you," I snarl, fighting to get free.

"Chill the fuck out, man. We're on your side. You want blood, we'll go get some. Just talk to me first," Marco says.

I lift my head and smack the back of it down on the wooden floorboard. Smack it again.

"She kick you out?"

I smack it harder. "When I tell you to not talk about her, I mean it," I rage. I can't seem to get free of my two cousins, who are determined to hold me down.

"What the fuck is going on?" Leo demands.

"His girl," Marco non-explains. He looks at me. "What happened? You piss her off?"

The rage seeps out of me, and I'm back to being the hollow man. Worse than ever, though. I try to swallow, trying to shuffle through the jumble of images in my mind.

The pregnancy test.

Hannah's pinched face. Her tears.

I'm cracking. I can't do this anymore.

"I pushed her away," I croak, sickened by the realization.

Marco's expression shows nothing. We both have perfected our masks. "You can't fix it?"

"No," I rasp. "I can't be what she needs. An entire gang wants me dead. I'm a goddamn danger to her."

Marco continues to look at me passively. "So we fix that."

I stare back. If that problem were gone, could I be what Hannah needed?

The sickness in my stomach resurfaces.

Not even fucking close.

I'm nothing. I've got nothing to offer. I don't even know who the fuck I am anymore. I have no life, nothing.

I close my eyes, all the remaining fight leaving my body. "No."

"No?" Marco demands, challenge in his voice.

"No," I say firmly. "I can't be that guy for her."

"I'll tell you one thing," Marco says, climbing off me. Leo follows. He clasps palms with me and hauls me to my feet. "The Mando I know figures shit out when he wants something."

I stare at him. Resentment burns in my gut. Now that I'm feeling emotions again, I'd like to set the whole fucking city on fire. "The Mando you know is dead," I tell him and walk out the door.

"Hold up, man. You still want to pound someone's face in?"

I stop. Crack my knuckles. "Fuck, yeah."

"Let's go. I have a visit to pay."

Chapter Twenty-Four

Hannah

I go to my parent's house for Sunday dinner. I thought about canceling, but I'm actually hoping my mom will somehow know the right thing to say to fix me. She's good like that sometimes.

I cried for five days straight. I can't stop the waterworks to save my life. I've always been a crier, and I know the hormones don't help, but it's ridiculous.

Last week, I tried to run my shop and interact with people and put arrangements together, and the whole time, I had tears falling down my face. Josie had to come in and take over the last two days, so I could stay home with my head under the covers.

I walk in without knocking. My mom stands at the counter, throwing together a salad. I sink down in a kitchen chair, too exhausted to even go over and give her a hug.

"Hannah? What's wrong, baby?" My mom rushes over and envelopes me in one of those mom hugs that usually makes everything better.

I cry into her shoulder. "I'm pregnant," I blurt. "And I broke up with Armando."

She squeezes me even tighter. "Oh, baby." Her hand rubs circles on my back.

"I'm sorry, Mom." She drilled it into me young to use birth control until I was married and ready to start a family, but I had to go and fuck it up.

"Don't you worry about me," she says. "Let's worry about you, sweetheart. This is a lot."

"It is." A fresh spate of sobs come on.

"Hey, *hey*." She gives me a little shake. "This is big. But you know you're going to be okay, don't you? No matter how things turn out?"

I sniff and nod into her shoulder. "I can't tell if I made a mistake," I say between sniffs and sobs.

"Ending things with Armando?"

"Yeah." I pull away and wipe beneath my eyes. "But he was breaking my heart, you know? He said he couldn't be my boyfriend because he was too messed up."

My mom studies me, concern etched in the lines of her face. "Well, you're allowed to change your mind."

Fresh tears gush down my cheeks.

"What's going on—" my dad says from the doorway, but my mom waves him away, and he quickly retreats.

"I don't know, Mom. It just hurts so bad. I thought I would feel strong by ending things. I did feel strong while I did it. But now, I'm just a mess."

"Yeah," my mom says softly. "Breakups are never easy, even when they're the right decision."

My head snaps up, stomach tightening into a cruel knot. "Do you think it was the right decision?"

"I didn't say that," she cautions. "I don't know what the

right answer is. But I do know one thing. You're smart and strong. And you have a huge heart. And I know you're going to be able to figure this out successfully."

I stare at her in despair. I want to believe her, but success feels completely impossible right now. I would settle for being able to turn off the water works for five minutes.

"What do I do about Armando?" I whisper, even though I know my mom, and she's not going to give me the answer.

"Well, I'll tell you one thing. If you keep this baby, there'll be no getting rid of him. When you have a baby with a man, he's in your life for the rest of your days whether the two of you are together or apart. Unless he chooses to walk away from his responsibility."

"What if he never finds out?" I croak, knowing how wrong it is but still clinging to the idea.

"What?"

"I wasn't going to tell him about the baby," I admit in a whisper.

"Why not?" My mom's voice sharpens.

I suck in a terraced breath. "Well, when he saw the test box, he freaked out. So I know he really doesn't want it. That's when I told him to leave. And I just lied and said the test came out negative."

I sense the censure from my mom as she draws in a slow breath. "So let me get this straight. You broke up with him because he didn't react the way you wanted him to when he was surprised by the idea of a pregnancy?"

I pull my lower lip into my mouth and suck on it. It sounds a little extreme when she puts it that way. "He's emotionally unavailable," I assert.

My mom nods slowly. "That may very well be, but it

sounds to me like he was experiencing *some* emotion. Stress, maybe? Which is healthy. Because having a pregnancy you didn't expect is a big deal."

Well, *yeah*.

I wipe some more tears. "What should I do?"

"Well, the better question is what do you think you should do?"

I freaking hate when she says things like that. I shake my head. "I don't know."

My mom nods. "I think you probably do."

My chest aches as I realize my mom calls bullshit on my *I don't knows,* same as Armando, only nicer.

All the ways he paid attention to me flood my mind. He may have claimed he had nothing to offer, but it wasn't true. He took care of me. He noticed when I was off or mad and didn't let it slide. He tried to fix things when they were broken.

And what had I done?

Run away from my problems, same as ever. Opted to not deal with them.

I bailed. On him. On us.

Maybe if I'd given him a chance, he would've risen to the occasion of being a dad. It's hard to imagine he would stop taking care of me.

And then I'm suddenly bone tired.

I scrub my hands over my cheeks and stand. "I don't think I can stay for dinner, Mom," I say. "Please don't tell Dad about what's going on with me yet. I need to figure stuff out."

My mom glances toward the living room and gives me a noncommittal shrug. "He may have already heard enough, but I'll leave it for you to share." She wraps me in another hug. "I love you, baby girl. Nothing's insurmountable. Remember that."

I nod. "Love you, Mom."

Chapter Twenty-Five

Armando

The evening sky is painted with hues of orange and pink as I trudge up the steps to my apartment, the weight of a long day pressing down on me like a heavy cloak. As soon as I unlock the door and step inside, my thoughts drift towards Hannah. Her laughter echoes in my mind like a melody, her presence soothing my weary soul. But the danger lurking beneath the surface—the darkness that threatens to consume us both—casts an unshakeable shadow over my heart.

I collapse onto the bed, not bothering to change out of my clothes and allow sleep to claim me. But instead of finding refuge in the warmth of slumber, I'm thrust into a nightmare that chills me to the core.

I'm standing in the middle of an abandoned warehouse, the air thick with tension and fear. The walls loom high above me, like ancient guardians of some forsaken realm, while shadows dance across the cracked concrete floor. My heart races, each beat pounding against my chest as if trying to break free from its cage.

"Where am I?" I whisper, my voice barely audible above the eerie silence.

A sudden gust of wind sends shivers down my spine, and I wrap my arms around myself for comfort, but it's no use. I can't shake the feeling that something isn't right, that some malevolent force has trapped me here in this desolate place.

"Armando," a familiar voice calls out, echoing through the vast emptiness.

Hannah. The sound of her voice sets off a flare of panic within me, igniting every protective instinct I possess. I need to find her, to make sure she's safe from the dangers that have haunted my past and now threaten our future.

"Where are you?" I call out desperately, my voice cracking with the strain of emotion.

"Help me, Armando," she pleads, her voice distant and muffled by the oppressive darkness.

I grit my teeth, my resolve hardening like steel. No matter what it takes, I will find her and protect her from the shadows of my past that have come to claim us both. With each step I take, determination courses through my veins, fueling my need to save the woman who has captured my heart and awakened a fierce love within me.

Hannah's muffled cries grow louder, guiding me through the darkness. My heart hammers against my chest, my breath coming in ragged gasps as I navigate the maze-like structure of this forsaken warehouse. The air hangs heavy and oppressive around me, a tangible weight on my shoulders that I struggle to shake off.

"Armando!" she calls out again, her voice wavering with fear.

"Keep talking, Hannah," I shout back, my words dripping with desperation. "I'm coming for you."

"Please... hurry," she whispers, the sound barely reaching my ears.

I push myself harder, sprinting through the labyrinth of shadows and echoes, each turn revealing another dead end or empty corridor. But I refuse to give up, driven by the knowledge that Hannah's life depends on me finding her.

"Armando... I'm so scared," she admits, her voice cracking under the weight of her terror.

"Stay strong, Hannah," I plead, my own fear seeping into my words. "I'll find you. I promise."

Finally, after what feels like an eternity, I reach a dimly lit room at the heart of the warehouse. And there, tied to a chair in the center of the space, is Hannah. Naked, vulnerable, and trembling with fear, her eyes lock onto mine, wide and pleading.

"Armando," she gasps, tears streaming down her cheeks. "You found me."

"I'm here," I say, my voice strained with relief and determination. "I won't let anything happen to you."

As I move closer, I can see the ropes biting into her skin, leaving angry red welts across her wrists and ankles. My fingers fumble with the knots, my urgency making the task more difficult than it should be.

"Who did this to you?" I ask, trying to keep my voice steady as I work to free her.

"I don't know," she admits, her eyes darting around the room as if searching for answers. "They kept their faces hidden."

"Once I get you out of here, we'll make sure they never hurt you again," I promise, my hands shaking with anger and fear.

"Do you really think we can escape them?" Her voice is barely a whisper.

"Fuck yes," I reply, forcing confidence into my words even as doubt gnaws at the edges of my mind. *"I won't let anyone or anything come between us. Not now, not ever."*

A faint smile flickers across her lips, her eyes shining with love and trust despite the terror that still lingers in their depths. And in that moment, I vow to myself that no matter what it takes, I will protect this woman–the one who has brought light back into my darkened world and given me a reason to fight for a better future.

"Thank you," she whispers.

"Always, Flowers. Always," I reply, my heart swelling with determination as I finally untie the last knot, setting her free from her bonds.

As I step closer to Hannah, the air around us seems to thicken, as if charged with an impending storm. The hairs on the back of my neck rise, and a shiver of dread snakes down my spine. Without warning, the warehouse is filled with the low murmur of voices–voices that I recognize all too well.

"Armando," Hannah whispers, her eyes wide with fear. "Who are they?"

"Stay quiet," I urge her, my voice barely audible. I can feel their presence closing in around us, like vultures circling their prey.

"Long time no see, Mando," one of them sneers, stepping out from the shadows. His grin is cruel, his eyes cold and calculating. I recognize him as one of my former mafia associates, a man I had hoped never to cross paths with again.

"Leave her alone," I growl, positioning myself between Hannah and the menacing figures. My heart hammers against my ribcage, but I refuse to let them see any signs of weakness. My dark world has found me, but I'll be damned if I let it take away the only person who truly matters to me.

"Ah, so this is the girl who's got you so whipped, huh?" another one chimes in, leering at Hannah. "You should have known we'd find you eventually, Armando."

I glance over my shoulder, locking eyes with Hannah. Her gaze is filled with terror, but there's also a flare of determination there. As if she's silently urging me to fight back.

"Get away from her," I snarl, my fists clenching at my sides. With every fiber of my being, I want to protect Hannah—to shield her from these monsters and the horrors that they represent.

As if sensing my resolve, the men lunge forward, their faces twisted with malice and vengeance. I throw myself into the fray, fists flying as I slam them into the first attacker. The impact jolts through my arm, but it only fuels my adrenaline.

"Armando!" Hannah cries out, her voice strangled with fear.

"Stay back!" I shout, desperation clawing at my insides as I struggle to keep the attackers at bay.

But they just keep coming—too many for me to handle alone. Their numbers give them an advantage that I can't overcome, no matter how fiercely I fight. Blow after blow rains down upon me, each one landing with brutal precision.

Pain flares through my body, but it's nothing compared to the agony of knowing that these men are here because of me—because of the life I led before I met Hannah. My past has caught up with me, and now she's the one who will pay the price.

"Armando," she whispers, her eyes filled with love and trust even as tears stream down her cheeks. "Tonight's the night I die."

. . .

I wake up wanting to die. It's the fourth fucking night in a row I dreamt about Hannah. Nightmares. Always with her in danger because of me. About to be killed. Tortured, screaming my name. All to hurt me. This time it was at Lollipops. She was there but tied to a chair, naked.

Like it was the guys in the Outfit who wanted to hurt her and not some street gang.

She was screaming my name, begging—not for them to leave her alone but for them not to kill me.

I don't know where I was in the dream. There, but unable to help. My limbs wouldn't move. My mouth couldn't speak. I tried to shout, to fight, but nothing happened.

I roll off the bed. I'm still in my clothes from yesterday, soaked with sweat, reeking of whiskey.

Since the night Hannah broke up with me, I've drunk myself to sleep every night, but alcohol does little to numb the sensation of having my heart cut out with a chainsaw. Everything swirls around me like a fog.

I pull off my clothes and step into the shower. All week, I've tempted fate. I've been at my apartment. Gone to my job. Walk in broad daylight. Done everything I can to fucking dare the Hermanos to find me, but my deathwish isn't answered.

I just want to get things settled. Kill or be killed.

Then, maybe, I'll find my way out of the dark.

My phone rings while I'm in the shower, and I shut off the water and step out to get it.

"Luis."

"Hey, I talked to one of the Hermanos. It's not about the guy you ended in prison—they don't seem to care about that. Word is a few of them are working for hire. Nothing personal."

Nothing personal.

"You found out who hired it?"

"Nah. Guy I talked to didn't know. I'll keep trying, though."

"Yeah. Thanks."

"Uh huh. You good for this?"

"How much do I owe you?"

"Seven hundred."

It's seven hundred bucks for not a lot of info, but I don't complain. "I'll drop it by."

"Cool." He ends the call, and I stand there, dripping.

All I can think about is Hannah. I *have* to clear this fucking contract.

For her.

Even if she never wants to see me again.

Even if we never talk, never touch again.

Chapter Twenty-Six

Armando

The dimly lit bar feels like an extension of the night outside as we push through the heavy doors. The air is thick with cigarette smoke and the low hum of murmured conversations.

"Scotch, neat," I order gruffly, my voice strained, betraying the turmoil I've been trying my damnedest to hide.

Marco and Leo exchange concerned glances.

"Make it three," Marco adds, his voice steady and strong.

The bartender nods in acknowledgment, placing three glasses before us. The amber liquid catches what little light filters through the smoky haze, casting a warm glow over the worn wooden table.

I waste no time, grabbing my drink and downing it in one swift motion. The clink of glass against wood punctuates the moment, and it occurs to me I'm seeking solace at the bottom of a glass. I've never been that man before.

Maybe I'm that man now.

"Are you all right, man?" Marco asks. "You look like shit."

"Fine," I reply tersely, but the way my hands grip the edge of the table tells a different story.

"Talk to us, man," Leo urges. "We're here for you."

"Like I said, I'm fine," I insist, but my voice wavers ever so slightly, revealing the cracks in my armor.

"How are you holding up after everything with Hannah?" Marco asks, his voice gentle and concerned. His gaze is steady and sincere, a softness in it that I've rarely seen.

I take a deep breath, knowing that I can't avoid this conversation any longer. "It's hard," I admit, my voice cracking slightly. "But it's for the best. She asked me to leave, and I can't blame her. I've been trying to get her out of my head since. And epically failing at it."

"Hey, don't be so hard on yourself," Marco replies, placing a reassuring hand on my shoulder.

"Enough about me," I say, trying to change the subject. "How's your ass, *cugino*?" It's a weak attempt at humor, but I'm desperate to steer the conversation away from my own pain.

Marco chuckles, shaking his head. "You're really gonna ask me about that now? Fine, it hurts like hell at times, but I'll live."

"You get asked about your ass on the daily now," Leo chimes in, rolling his eyes. "That ass of yours is becoming famous."

"Don't be jealous of my famous ass," Marco retorts with a smirk, before turning back to me. "But seriously, Mando, we're here for you, man. If you need to talk, just let us know."

"Thanks," I mumble, taking another swig of my drink. It

burns going down, but I welcome the sensation–anything to help numb the ache inside me.

As the warmth of the alcohol spreads through my chest, I can't help but think of Hannah. Of her smile, her laughter, the way she made me feel alive again. But that life is gone now, and all that's left is the cold, hard reality of my past.

"I have to be frank with you, man," Leo says, leaning forward with a serious expression. "You're a fucking fighter. Always have been. You don't just give up on shit so easily, man. Why the fuck would you just walk away? You obviously care about this chick. So why the fuck are you here with us instead of demanding her back?"

I stare into my glass, the amber liquid swirling around as I contemplate his words. The truth is, walking away was the hardest thing I've ever done. But what choice did I have?

"I didn't want to walk away," I confess, the weight of my emotions threatening to overcome me. "But I can't risk hurting Hannah. Our life... it's dangerous. It'll catch up to us, and she'll be in the crosshairs. She deserves better than that."

"Deserves better?" Leo scoffs, clearly not buying my argument. "She deserves a man who loves her, and from what I've seen, that's you. Maybe it's time to stop running from your past and face it head-on. For her sake."

"Maybe you're right," I admit, my fingers tightening around my glass. "Maybe I need to confront my past if I want any shot at a future with Hannah. But where the fuck do I even begin?"

"You need to see her," Marco interjects. "Talk to her. Tell her everything you just told us–about your fears, your love, your willingness to fight for her. Then, together, you can figure out the best way to move forward."

"Maybe," I agree, my chest swelling with newfound

determination and even hope. My cousins may be right. I can't let Hannah go without a fight. She means too much to me.

"By walking away without a fight, you've already lost her. You had something special with Hannah, and you just let it go," Marco says.

"Marco's right," Leo adds, leaning forward in the booth. "You didn't even put up a fight for your relationship. We all have our demons, but that doesn't mean we can't fight for love."

I look at both of them, their expressions a mixture of frustration and empathy. My chest feels tight, my thoughts consumed by the memory of Hannah's face when I walked out her door.

"Remember when we were kids?" I ask, trying to change the subject. "Alter boys, all three of us. Who would've thought we'd end up where we are now?"

"Definitely not me," Marco chuckles, the mood lightening a bit. "But that's life, right? It's unpredictable."

"Damn straight," Leo agrees. "And you know what else is unpredictable? Love. But that doesn't mean we shouldn't fight for it."

"You're lucky," Marco says, his voice filled with sincerity. "I'd give anything to have more than just a fuck here and there. You and Hannah have something real. Don't throw it away like it's nothing."

"Besides," Leo chimes in, smirking as he swirls the ice in his drink, "you've always been one stubborn bastard. Why give up so easily?"

I can't help but smile at their words, knowing they both have a point. They've been with me through thick and thin, and they've never steered me wrong.

"All right, all right," I concede, my resolve beginning to

strengthen. "Maybe I did walk away too quickly. Maybe I should've fought harder."

"Damn right." Marco nods, his eyes meeting mine with determination. "Now it's up to you to fix it."

"Good man." Leo grins, raising his glass in a toast. "To fighting for love and finding our way back home."

"*Salute*," Marco and I echo, clinking our glasses together before drinking, the alcohol burning like liquid courage.

Despite the growing warmth in my chest, uncertainty still gnaws at me. I can't shake the feeling that I'm walking a tightrope between love and destruction. My cousins' words have given me hope, but they haven't fully convinced me.

"All right," I finally say, forcing myself to sound more confident than I feel. "I'll stop moping around. But I need to think this through before I take any action."

"Fair enough," Marco acknowledges, his eyes narrowing as he studies me. "Just don't wait too long, okay? We both know women like Hannah can be snatched up in seconds."

"Believe me, I know," I mutter, my thoughts turning from pity to rage. The thought of her being with another man sends homicidal thoughts through me. "I'll think on it."

"Good," Leo grins, his mood shifting as he claps his hands together. "Now, let's lighten up the atmosphere a bit, shall we?"

"Agreed," Marco chuckles, raising his glass. "To not having bullets in our asses!"

The absurdity of the toast pulls a half-hearted chuckle from me, and I hold my own glass up to join theirs. "Amen to that."

Our glasses clink together with a satisfying sound, and for a moment, I allow myself to forget about the weight on my shoulders. We drink to our shared camaraderie–three cousins bound by blood, loyalty, and the ghosts of our pasts.

As the night wears on, the conversation drifts away from Hannah and back to lighter subjects. I appreciate my cousins' attempts to distract me, but I can't help but feel the persistent tug of my thoughts pulling me back to her.

I let her go.

I fucked up.

But it wouldn't be the first time I sabotaged my life.

The question now is what will I do next? Continue to dig my grave, or fucking walk toward the light that is Hannah?

Chapter Twenty-Seven

Hannah

The next week, I drag myself back into work, but I'm wearing Armando's faded Cubs t-shirt—the one with a hole near the collar. It was in my hamper because I'd slipped it on after having sex one night, so he didn't pack it when he left.

I don't know why I put it on today—to torture myself? It really makes no sense.

I've really been thinking over what my mom said to me.

Maybe I was hasty in breaking up with Armando. Certainly not telling him about the baby was wrong. I knew that even before my mom let her judgment bleed through. But hearing it reflected back at me brought it home.

I've been feeling like the injured party, maybe because my heart's so damn sore, but really, I'm the one who caused this pain. For both of us, assuming Armando's also grieving.

I flip open the wedding arrangement album and price list and push it across the counter. I'm helping a couple order flowers for their wedding. It's only the third wedding order I've taken since I took over the shop, so despite my low spirits, I'm thankful. The somewhat bored groom-to-be looks familiar. I'm pretty sure he's one of the mafia guys who gets their hair cut next door. So it seems greasing that wheel is working.

Thank-fucking-god.

"I heard you're an award-winning florist," the bride-to-be says, looking around.

I flush, wondering if the place looks like an award-winning shop. Also, wondering where the hell she heard such a thing. But screw that, my arrangements are good—damn good. Better than Mary Alice's. And I have a decent shot at winning an award in that competition in a couple months. I square my shoulders.

"We like to keep things fresh and original here. I put a lot of thought into my arrangements to make them fit the individual—or the couple."

I kick myself for not updating the arrangement book with designs of my own—the photos are still Mary Alice's. But I go off-book and start offering what I can see this couple using. "What color are your bridesmaids wearing?"

"Black cocktail dresses of their own choosing," she says.

"Evening wedding?"

"Yes."

"So you could do almost anything with the flowers. Do you have favorites?"

Her eyes sweep around the place again. "Roses, I guess," she says.

"Roses are classic, of course. White or red would be the most formal, or you could do any other color that's a favorite."

The bride looks uncertain.

"Or you could do something totally unique. Mix something exotic in with roses. Like shades of pink and blush old fashioned roses with peonies. Or star-gazer lilies."

She brightens. "Yes, something unique sounds great. I'd love the peonies."

I talk her through the order, suggesting possibilities for table arrangements, altar, decorations, bridesmaids, groomsmen and, of course, her bouquet. At the end, we come up with a package close to $2500, which the guy doesn't seem to blink at.

"So how did you hear about us?" I ask, hoping I sound casual. Forcing myself to make an attempt at being personable, even though I don't feel like it.

"Armando Rossi," the bride says.

When I start, she goes still, her eyes slowly traveling from my face down to my chest. No, to the t-shirt. "Wait, are you... *dating* Armando?" she asks incredulously.

Shock flashes through me, mirrored in both her eyes and —strangely—those of her fiancé.

I blink rapidly. Dammit. I made it all day without a tear. "Ah..." I don't even know what to say. My stomach turns queasy again.

Why I didn't realize that, of course, Armando was the one who told them I was award-winning. Who else?

And then further realization sinks in. I gasp. "Are you *Grace*?"

She stares at me with bald curiosity. "You're dating him. Wow. I didn't see that one coming."

Her fiancé frowns. "You and Armando?" he demands, wagging a finger from me to my cell phone.

"No. Well, we were. But it's..."

I don't know why it feels so wrong to say *no*. I want to claim Armando as mine in front of these people. In front of his ex-girlfriend and her new fiancé. Maybe it's to help restore Armando's pride, maybe mine. I'm not sure.

"It's complicated. But yes," I answer, lifting my chin.

"Whoa. Okay. Sorry, I didn't mean to make this awkward," Grace says. "Armando told me I should come here to order the flowers for my wedding, but he didn't let on that you two were an item. Congratulations. I mean, I'm really glad for him. For you both."

My stomach churns at the lie. At wishing we had something to be glad for.

Strangely, I think she means it.

Her boyfriend looks at me with a cool, assessing gaze that unnerves me. Like, what the heck is he trying to figure out?

My hand drops protectively to my abdomen, and his gaze tracks the movement.

I clear my throat. "The total on your deposit is $1348," I say.

"Sure, doll." Emilio pulls out a wad of cash with that swagger that I'm used to seeing from my mafioso customers and peels off fourteen hundred dollar bills. "Keep the change and give my lady a nice bouquet, all right? Whatever she wants." He turns to Grace. "I'm gonna step outside and make a phone call, doll." He leans in to kiss her cheek.

I'm turned off by the fact that he calls us both *doll*. I sort of instantly hate him for hurting Armando although that's irrational. If he hadn't stolen Grace away, Armando might still be with her. And that would leave me without ever experiencing what it meant to be consumed by a man like him. To swim in his intensity.

"I'll make you something special," I tell Grace because there's no one else in the shop, and I can spare a few minutes to throw something together that she'll love. I'm still trying to impress her, despite the fact that she broke Armando's heart.

Despite the fact that I may have smashed what was left of it after she finished.

"I'll be right back."

I have the back door to the alley propped open to let the breeze through because it's cool for once, and I hear the boyfriend talking on his cell phone.

"Call it off. Yeah, I'm sure. I'm rescinding the job. It's off. No money will be paid."

A shiver sidles up my spine. I'm certain that's a conversation I shouldn't be overhearing. Not wanting to once again become a witness to something illegal, I hurry to finish the arrangement and rush back to the lobby with the vase in hand.

"Here you go." I force a smile, still fighting off the sense of foreboding from hearing that phone call and the ache of having all my feelings for Armando activated once more.

"Thank you." She studies me with curiosity. "Can I ask how you and—never mind." She shakes her head. "It's none of my business. I'm just happy for you guys."

If only happiness could be ours.

"Thanks." I watch her walk out before I pick up my phone and pull up an old text from Armando. He hasn't texted once since I kicked him out.

I don't know why I thought he would. But some part of me must've hoped because every day that goes by without hearing from him makes me die a little more.

My thumb hovers over my screen trying to decide if I should initiate communication. Finally, I settle for, *Thanks for recommending me to Grace.*

Then I delete the whole thing. If I send it, he might call and I'm not sure I can handle talking to him.

Still, I want to thank him. I can't imagine he enjoyed talking to her. I just can't picture him chatting her up in any way. So that fact that he stuck his neck out to make sure she got her flowers here means something. Whether it was before or after we broke up, I don't know, but either way, it was nice of him.

And that's when I'm sure.

I made a terrible mistake.

Chapter Twenty-Eight

Armando

Larry's happy, I'm finally doing what I was supposed to on this job—sit back and do nothing while the rest of them work.

I rub my swollen knuckles and stare at Hannah's dad, who's back on the job already. I was on edge, ready to fuck Larry in the ass with my boot if he gave Harold any shit about being out, but nothing happened.

Harold refuses to look at me, and Larry tries to pretend I'm not here anyway.

The last week has been a fucking blur. I go out every night with Marco and Leo delivering messages for the don then losing my mind in a bottle. The days are nothing. I don't even know how they pass. It's like being in prison again. One minute bleeds into an hour bleeds into a day. Nothing but violence and staying alive to fuel my existence.

At quarter 'til five o'clock, everyone starts moving in unison, packing their shit up to go. I stand and start to head out, but I see Harold looking over at me.

I wait because—fuck—I'm desperate for any kind of

news about Hannah, any kind of connection to her. I've been so fucking lost without her. Dead.

He walks toward me like he's pissed. With intent. Like he's going to punch me in the gut.

And when he reaches me, he does.

I take it like a man, and I don't fight back because he's Hannah's fucking dad. If he thinks I deserve his wrath, he's probably right.

He hits me again, this time in the ribs. Then once more in the jaw.

"I don't care who the fuck you are. Or what family you work for. If you think you're gonna knock up my daughter and walk away, you'd better think again."

It takes a second for his words to sink in. *Knock up*. He said *knock*. *Up*.

I swipe the blood from my lip with the back of my hand. "Hannah's pregnant?" I demand.

The guy goes still, like he realized he might have fucked up. Like maybe I wasn't supposed to know.

I remember that pregnancy test box on the table. She told me it had been negative.

She lied?

Why?

A dozen scenarios run through my mind, but I don't stop to ask Harold, who obviously doesn't know what's going on in his daughter's head any more than I do. I leave him standing there and jog to the street. I need a fucking Uber.

Right fucking now!

For once in my goddamn life, things seem to go my way because a taxi pulls over when I flag it, and I throw myself inside, giving the address for Garden of Eden.

She lied and broke up with me rather than telling me she was pregnant. Why? *Why?*

Because she knew I'd be no good as a father and provider was the most obvious answer. That was the reason I'd freaked out when I saw the test box. And because I already had someone who wanted me dead, and I sure as hell didn't need to endanger a tiny innocent life with my fucked up drama.

Something uneasy twists in my gut as I replay my reaction. What if she lied because of how I acted? My sensitive, beautiful flower. She feels every emotion I should've been feeling. She's like a conduit for them. Maybe she felt my dismay and shut me out because of it. Maybe she thought I'd pressure her to get an abortion or some shit.

Fanculo! I failed her in every fucking way! I completely botched the pregnancy test in addition to my refusal to show up the way she needed me to. To be her man. To offer a genuine partnership.

Fuck! It's all I can do not to punch the hell out of the taxicab door, but I restrain myself. I can't get kicked out of the cab—not before I get to Garden of Eden.

And I don't even know what the hell I'm going to do or say to win her back. I still don't have a solution to my life-threatening shitshow. All I know is that I'm sure as hell going to fight for her.

For us.

I fucked things up big time, but that doesn't mean it's irreparable.

At least, I really fucking hope not.

Chapter Twenty-Nine

Hannah

The store is empty as usual when my phone rings at the shop. I pick it up where I'm putting together arrangements in the back.

When I see who's calling, I'm slightly alarmed. "Daddy?" He never calls me. It's always Mom who reaches out. I know my dad loves me, but he's definitely the strong, silent type.

Like Armando.

Dammit, why does everything remind me of Armando?

"Hey baby. Listen, I know you have something personal going that you aren't ready to tell me—"

"Daddy, please. I'm at work. I don't want to talk about it now." I blink quickly to clear my already smarting eyes and jockey an alstroemeria around in the bouquet until it sits right.

"I know, I know—that's okay," he says in a rush. "I heard enough when you came over to put together that you're pregnant and broke things off with that boyfriend of yours."

I stop arranging and hold my breath. Suck it in like I

was punched in the gut, and it stays in, suspended. quivering.

"Well, I probably shouldn't have said anything to him..."

I gasp. Why hadn't I considered the fact that my dad and Armando still work together? "What'd you say?" I lay the rose in my fingers down on the counter, unable to continue.

"Hannah, you're not in any danger from that man, are you?" he asks sharply.

"From *Armando*?" I demand with exaggerated skepticism. "No. *He's* in danger from some gang, but no. He would never hurt me."

"Okay. But he doesn't know? I mean, he does now... I'm sorry, baby. It was pissing me off watching him show up hungover every day and not giving two fucks about the job when I knew you were crying your eyes out over this."

I swallow. "He was hung over?" That doesn't sound like him. It's stupid to think it might be because of me, but my foolish heart wants to.

"I'm pretty sure he's on his way over there now. I just wanted to give you a heads up."

"Okay, thanks," I whisper and close my eyes as I slowly lower the phone, my heart flopping wildly in my chest. Hope and anxiety overlap, weave together, turn me inside out. Rational thought flees. I try to recount the reasons I didn't tell him. The reasons it was important to stay broken up, but they disappear.

I hear the bells I wrapped around the door handle to let me know when someone enters, jingle, and I step out to the front, my pulse racing. The moment I see his haggard face, I hiccup-sob and cover my mouth.

"Hannah." His voice is gruff as he crosses the floor of the shop in a few swift steps and comes around behind the counter. He's going to wrap me up in his arms. I sense his intent as strongly as I sense his angst, his strength, his determination.

"Don't," I plead, holding out a hand to stop him. Because once I'm in his arms again, I will never have the strength to push him away. I'll never have the will to end things. It will feel too right. I already know that. "I'm trying to get over you," I choke out.

"Please," he rasps. "I need to fucking hold you." His voice sounds like broken concrete and steel—wrecked but so damn strong.

And of course, there's no resisting him. I need him. I fall into his arms, and he pulls me against his muscled chest.

"I'm sorry, baby. I fucked everything up. Right from the start," he confesses to my hair, his lips moving the curls, his breath warm against my scalp. He doesn't ease the steel lockhold he has on my body, which is good because my legs stop working. "I didn't know going into this I was going to fall in love."

I stop breathing.

"I didn't know you'd become the fucking *heart* beating in my chest. All I knew was that you'd witnessed me kill a man and that made you a risk, but there was no way I could hurt you or even pretend I might hurt you. And all I could think to do was to take you home." His fingers slide under my hair, and he runs his thumb lightly over my nape. "Fuck, maybe I did know, even then. Because after that kiss, I never wanted to let you go. I wanted to tie you to my bedpost and keep you for-fucking-ever."

I realize I'm trembling all over. Incapable of speaking. I soak him in even though I resolved to be strong.

"Hannah." Now he eases the arm around me and pulls back, cupping my face. It's painful to look at him, but he waits until I do, and then I can't look away. I realize with a shock he has a bruise on his jaw and dark circles under his eyes.

"I fucked everything up, but if you give me a do-over, I swear to Christ you won't be sorry. I will figure out how to be your man." He leans his forehead against mine. "Please let me be your man."

I suck in a breath. "Are you here... because of what my dad told you?"

I don't know what I want him to say—there's so much packed into this, and it's all twisted together.

He hesitates like he wants to get the answer right but isn't sure how. "I want this baby—" he blurts suddenly, dropping his hands from my face and shoving them in his pockets. Giving me space. "I mean, if you do. I support you, no matter what. I'm sorry I freaked. It just scares the ever-loving shit out of me to think something might happen to either of you because of me. But I'm gonna solve that shit," he vows, his gaze steady. Firm. "I'm gonna solve it, and I will keep you safe. I promise you that."

It's the first time since he's been back I see that old confidence in him. The guy who sat on top of the world. Who knows what he wants and how to get it. Maybe Armando just needed a reason to give a damn about life on the outside.

Maybe I'm that reason.

"Hannah." His voice goes soft, and he steps in again, resting a hand lightly on my waist. "Give me another chance. Please. I'll get it right this time. I won't let you down." His other hand snakes around behind my head and tilts my face up. "And I want the baby. But no pressure."

His handsome face turns blurry from my tears. "I want

the baby, too," I whisper. "She can come to work with me. I mean, I'm my own boss. I can totally make this work."

His eyes crinkle, and the corners of his lips tug up slightly. Leave it to our unborn baby to be the first thing to make him truly smile. A real, toothy, honest to God smile. "*She?*"

I shrug. "Feels like it."

His lips stretch wider. "She'll be beautiful. Like you." His gaze roves lovingly over my face. "May I kiss you?"

I let out a little puff of air because he sounds like we're on a first date. "You're asking permission now?"

His eyes crinkle again. "I told you, I'm gonna do it right this time. If you'll have me." He leans forward and stops with his lips millimeters from mine. "Say you'll have me."

"I'll have you," I whisper then push him away, right before his lips crash down on mine. "But you *can't* break my heart," I warn.

He shakes his head. "I'm all in, Hannah. And when I commit, I'm loyal as hell. This time will be good, I swear."

I close the distance between our lips and kiss-attack him. He gives it back to me, like he always does, devouring my mouth, his tongue plundering, his lips taking, drinking.

"I love you, Flowers," he murmurs when we come up for air.

My vision goes blurry. "I love you, too."

Chapter Thirty

Armando

The thing with love is that it makes you miss things you should've caught. My mind zeroed in on seeing Hannah. I knew it was Friday, and the guys were next door, but I didn't spare them any notice when I walked by. Nor did I pay attention to the guy loitering across the street.

I was too consumed with getting to Hannah and fixing that shit.

When the door bells jingle, we break apart, and I see Lorenzo, one of the old-timers come in.

"Mando," he says, like he's surprised to find me behind the counter in a liplock with Hannah.

"Lorenzo. How's it going?" For the first time since I got out, I don't hate everyone. I'm almost glad to see a familiar face. Proud to show off my relationship. My beautiful, pregnant girlfriend.

"What's going on here? You and ah…" His curious gaze shifts between the two of us.

"Hannah," I fill in, guessing he doesn't know or

remember her name. "Yeah. This is my girl. Hannah, this is Lorenzo."

"I know Lorenzo," Hannah says with a laugh. "Two bouquets for you today?"

Lorenzo grins at her. "That's right. One for the wife and one for the *goomba*." He winks at me.

Hannah heads to the cooler. I realize she's wearing my Cubs shirt over her red short-shorts, and it floods my chest with warmth.

Feelings.

Feelings are fucking breaking through all over the place.

But that's when the shit hits the fan.

Gunshots ring out, and the front windows and glass doors shatter.

"Get down," I shout, lunging for Hannah and dragging her to the floor. Lorenzo draws a weapon but stays on the floor, crawling across the floor to where we are, behind the counter.

I'm usually cool as fuck in an emergency, but Hannah's here, with my unborn child. When the shots stop, I say to Lorenzo, "Get her out the back. Please." I take the gun from his hand because I don't have a weapon on me.

Lorenzo doesn't hesitate. He's a soldier, like me. He grabs Hannah's arm, hauls her up and books it for the back door. Glass from the windows falls in the eerie silence after the deafening shots.

"Lorenzo," I call out, and he turns at the door. "Make *sure* she's taken care of... if I don't make it out."

"No!" Hannah screams, and Lorenzo has to wrap his arms around her to keep her from running back to me.

"And my mom. Promise me." I cock the gun.

"You have my word."

"*Lorenzo*" —It seems so fucking important to say— "She's pregnant."

"*Lo prometo*," Lorenzo says in Italian with the reverence of swearing an oath, and then he hauls Hannah out the back door.

I suck in a breath and flatten my back against the wall just behind the counter.

More glass breaks, and I hear the crunch of footsteps over glass.

"Armando," someone sings. "Come out, come out, wherever you are."

This is it.

This is where I die. Right when I found a reason to live. When I'm needed. To think I could leave Hannah and our child before we even got a chance rips my goddamn lungs out.

But I also can't go on hiding. I can't have her or our baby in danger because I have a price on my head. This ends now. Tonight.

I check the magazine of the pistol to count how many shots I have then swallow back the bile in my throat. In the reflection of the cooler door, I see three of them. I can take them all.

"Drop your fucking weapons, or we'll mop the motherfucking floor with your blood."

My heart double pumps. *Arturo*. Many footsteps. The guys would've been next door for Friday haircuts. *La famiglia. My* family.

I step away from the wall, my own gun leveled at the guy closest to me. Arturo, Marco, Leo and Emilio are all there, guns leveled at the backs of the three gang members' heads.

"Nice and slow," Arturo says. "I don't know what the

fuck you think you're doing, but no one messes with a Pachino. You touch one hair on his head, Don Pachino will erase the existence of every one of you—every gang member, your mothers, your brothers, your sisters, and your fucking dogs—from the streets of this city."

"Easy man." I recognize the voice of the guy who called my name when he came in. He holds his gun out by the handle and slowly lowers it to the ground. His two friends do the same. "You don't know what you're talking about, man. The order came from Don Pachino. He hired us for this shit."

My body flushes with ice. The fuck?

"Bullshit," Arturo says immediately.

The guy slowly turns around. "Tell them." He lifts his chin at Emilio, whose eyes dart all over the fucking place.

Arturo sends a quick look at Emilio. *"Tell us what, Emilio?"* His voice is deadly. It makes goosebumps stand up on my arms.

"He hired us," the guy says.

"I called it off, asshole," Emilio grits through clenched teeth. Sweat beads at his forehead. He's as pale as a fucking Swede.

The ripple of shock that runs through the wise guys is palpable.

"I called it off today." Emilio shifts from foot to foot.

The guy shrugs. "I didn't get no memo."

"I called it off!" Emilio shouts, like he's losing his fucking head.

"You heard him," Arturo says, picking up the thread. "And that fucking order didn't come from the don. So if you don't want your entire gang obliterated, I suggest you walk out of here and never come near any of us again. *Capito?*"

"Yeah, okay." The guy tries to sound cool, but he and his two buddies exit swiftly.

The sound of sirens approaching fills the air, and Arturo curses. "Give me the fucking gun," he says to me because if I get caught with the thing, I'm gonna get another five years in the pen, just like that.

But I'm not about to give up my weapon. Not when there's a fucking traitor in our midst. I point it at Emilio's head. Marco and Leo do the same.

Emilio holds both hands in the air, his gun dangling on his trigger finger. Slowly, he drops to his knees and places the Walther PPK on the floor. "I thought you were going to kill me, Mando," he croaks. "Because of Grace." His hands visibly shake, but he holds eye contact with me, which is pretty fucking ballsy, considering he's admitting to putting a hit on me.

"You fucking bastard," Marco spits.

"I was afraid of you. Everyone thought you'd do something to me. Everyone, right?" He looks around for support, but no one says a fucking word. The cops screech up, lights flashing.

"Enough," Arturo snaps. "The don will settle this. Not any of you," he says fiercely, throwing his warning glance at me, Marco and Leo. "I mean it. He's a made man. You can't touch him. Don G. will decide his fate. Now give me that fucking gun, Mando, before you land your ass back in the can. Everyone else, put your goddamn pieces away. I'll handle the cops."

I put the safety on the gun and toss it to him as the cops advance. The rest of the guys put theirs away, and everyone raises their hands in the air. Emilio climbs awkwardly to his feet, never taking his gaze off me. He still thinks I'm going to kill him.

"They're gone," Arturo hollers to the cops. "It was some kind of gang hit, but they ran when we came out of the barbershop with our own weapons." He slowly walks outside, hands loosely held in the air. Don Pachino has some boys in blue on the payroll, and chances are good Artie knows who they are and vice versa. I can only fucking hope he can talk us out of this shit show.

I expect them to order us all face down, but they don't. They definitely know Artie. They let him approach and give them his story about what happened.

Marco purposely knocks into Emilio as he walks out, and Leo shoots him a look that swears death. I should be thinking about killing the bastard, but I don't. Because as I step outside, I see Hannah standing in front of Rocco's, tears streaming down her face. Lorenzo stands protectively by her side and nods to me when I lift my chin.

"Armando!" she cries out.

"It's okay, Flowers." I hold open my arms, and she runs into them. Her soft body collides with mine, she presses all those curves against me, buries her face in my chest. "It's over now. Forever."

She blinks up at me, and I stroke my thumb down her smooth brown skin. "It's over," I repeat, realizing it might be true.

Emilio revoked the hit. Arturo warned off the Hermanos who hadn't heard the message. That means other than the shit that needs to be resolved between me and Emilio, my life's safe for the moment.

My girl and our baby are safe.

I slide my fingers in her curls to cup the back of her head and meld my lips to hers. "Marry me?" I ask.

Her lips part in surprise. "Are you serious?"

"Dead serious, Flowers. You're the reason I want to

live. The reason I'm glad I'm free. Even without the baby, I'd want to move you into my place and keep you forever."

She lets out a watery laugh. "Wow. I don't know."

My heart stutters. I put a knuckle under her chin to lift her gaze to mine. "You don't know?"

"What about—" she flutters a hand at her ruined shop, the glass shattered from bullets.

I draw a breath and nod. "It's solved. I'm not a target anymore. And I swear to Christ I will not let anything like this touch you or our baby again."

She throws her arms around my waist and hugs me fiercely. "It's solved? Oh my God, Armando, that was horrible. I thought you were going to die."

"I know, beautiful. But it's over now, I promise."

She pulls away and lifts her face. *"Yes."*

I don't breathe. Is she saying *yes* to my proposal?

"Yes!" She nods vigorously as tears stream down her beautiful face.

"I love you." I look into her warm brown eyes when I say it. Hold her gaze, so she knows it's the goddamn truth. I'm her man, and I'm going to stand by her for life. Loyalty is my gig.

I look over to where Marco and Leo stand, sandwiching Emilio between them, like prison guards.

When Marco sees me looking, he mutters something and comes over, his curious gaze sweeping Hannah.

She swipes at her tears, wipes them on my shirt, letting out an embarrassed laugh.

"I hope you took him back. He's been a big baby since you kicked him out."

I don't even punch him because I'm too fucking happy. "Hannah just agreed to marry me."

Marco's face stretches into a grin. "That right? Congratulations!"

I hear Leo growl something like, "If you fucking run, I will hunt you down and eat your goddamn liver," to Emilio before he comes over and holds his hand out. "Did I just hear that right?"

"Yes," Hannah says with a watery laugh.

"She's now my fiancée," I fill in. "And she's having my baby."

"Whoa!" Marco grins.

Leo's brows wing up. "Way to lock it in, Mando."

There are smiles all around. Hell, I may even be smiling—that would be new.

"Mando." Hannah looks up at me under her curled lashes. "That's what they call you?"

I nod. "Yeah. Childhood nickname."

"I like it."

"I like you." I pull her against me and kiss the bridge of her nose.

Emilio stands and watches us, shoulders slouched, misery and fear lining his face. Frankly, I'm surprised he hasn't made a run for it, but he probably knows Leo told the truth. We would hunt him to the ends of the earth if he ran. Besides, he has a fiancée waiting at home for him.

Maybe he thinks he'll still make it out of this alive.

Arturo yells to Lorenzo in Italian to watch him, and I feel somewhat vindicated. It's not just Marco and Leo on my side. It's everyone.

I don't know what the don will do, but that current of loyalty, the strength of family that's been missing since I got out, turns back on. All but one of these men have my back.

It takes most of the sting away from knowing one of our own tried to buy my death.

Chapter Thirty-One

Hannah

"This is my place," Armando murmurs, opening the door to his apartment and flipping on the lights. His cousins, Marco and Leo both have apartments in the same building. I know because we all took the same elevator up.

After Armando called some friends in to clean the glass up at my place, he left someone in charge of staying all night to watch over the place until we can get the windows and door replaced tomorrow.

"It's nice," I say. It's way nicer than mine in terms of size and location although devoid of any personality.

"We could live here, if you want, because it's bigger. You can do whatever you want with it—make it colorful, like you."

I peer up at him. "You think I'm colorful?"

He turns to fully face me and wraps both arms around me. "Yeah." He brushes his lips over my nose. "Beautiful. Vibrant. Full of life." He glances at my belly, and his lips turn up. "Literally."

I love seeing the smile on his face. There are signs of fatigue around his eyes, but he looks more relaxed and happy than I've ever seen him. He told me on the way home that everything had been solved—there was no longer a hit out on him, and that it had been Emilio who put the contract out and hired the gang to execute it after Armando killed the first hitman. I told him about the phone call I overheard—how he must've canceled it after he learned we were a couple. I'm not saying that makes it all right—and I won't forgive Emilio for what he did—but it counts for something, I guess.

He leads me to the bedroom and gently pulls his shirt over my head. "I love seeing you in my clothes, Flowers," he rumbles, working the button on my shorts. He drops to a crouch, sliding his hands down my thighs as he pulls them down and off my legs. Then he stands and walks around me, trailing his fingertips lightly over my skin. It's so different from the rough way he usually takes me. He kisses across my shoulder, along the lines of my tattoo. "So beautiful," he murmurs.

Warmth floods my chest, making my breasts grow heavy, my nipples taut. I don't know if I'm sensing his emotions or my own—they're so intertwined. All the hard edges, the walls between us are gone now.

He moves behind me and unhooks my bra then cups my breasts, strumming my nipples with his thumbs. His teeth graze my neck. "That goomba shit with Lorenzo?" he says. "That's not me. I won't ever do that to you. I make a vow to you, Flowers, I'll keep it."

My heart picks up speed. This man is going to be my husband. Daddy to our child. I hadn't doubted him, but it's nice to hear him swear to be faithful. I lean my head back against his shoulder and cover his hands with my fingers.

He catches my wrists and pulls them above my head caged in one of his hands, lifting and spreading my breasts. With his other hand, he pinches my nipples, which are already hard as diamonds.

I moan softly. "They're tender," I complain.

He immediately stops. "Sorry, angel." He nuzzles his mouth against my jaw.

"No, don't stop. I like the way you touch me."

"Come here." He walks us both backward until we hit the bed and tumble to the springy mattress. After he pushes me to my back, his mouth descends on mine. The tenderness vanishes as raw hunger takes over. I tear his shirt off over his head. He knees my thighs apart. I unbutton his pants. He pulls off my panties. We are a wild tangle of lips and hands and melding bodies. I stroke my hands over his hard muscles, greedily touching everywhere I can—the bulging muscles of his arms, the ridges of his abdominals, the hard curve of his ass. He shucks his pants and slides into me unsheathed, his teeth sinking into the flesh of my neck.

I arch to take him deeper. "Yes."

"Yes," he echoes. He rocks into me with powerful surges. "Mine." He braces my shoulder to keep my head from hitting the headboard, but strokes my cheek with his thumb, a shred of tenderness still there. "You're mine now."

My lids flutter with the effort of keeping my eyes from rolling back with pleasure, but I lock my gaze with his. "I was yours from the beginning," I confess.

It's true. He didn't need to kidnap me and hold me captive. I would've gone with him anywhere. He had me with the first commanding touch.

"I love you," I tell him, never having to hold back those words again. He must know, though, because I'm incapable of hiding feelings.

Armando throws his head back, almost like he's in pain. He bares his teeth and roars, slamming into me hard, harder.

"Yes," I gasp. "Please."

Armando stills, his face taut with strain, his hands gouging my hips into the mattress as his cock swells inside me. He groans, his head falling forward, his arms coming around me to keep me close. "I love you," he whispers.

He thrusts deeper, and I gasp, loving the feeling of his enormous cock filling me to the brim and aching with need for more.

I lift my hand to stroke his cheek. His eyes close as he leans into my touch and kisses my palm.

"Forever mine," he whispers.

My heart swells.

He thrusts his cock even deeper. A tear leaks out of the corner of my eye, and Armando licks it away.

"Forever," I whisper.

"And always," he says, his thrusts slow and deep and perfect.

His cock throbs, the girth increases, and the heat intensifies.

The pleasure is so intense I can barely breathe. I'm being consumed. Consumed by his unending love. Is this solely my feelings, or am I also feeling his?

"Oh, Armando," I moan, the ecstasy so intense it feels like pain.

He moves faster, his cock slamming into me with such fervor I cry out. I don't know what's happening to me, but I can feel every ounce of raw, unadulterated emotion that courses through his body. It's like I can feel every emotion he has ever felt in his lifetime.

I can feel every old wound he has suffered, every time

someone he cared about hurt him, every time someone he trusted betrayed him. I can feel everything inside this man.

His fingers dig into the tender flesh of my hips, and he slams into me once more.

"Jesus, you feel so fucking good," he declares as he pounds into me. His lips move to my neck, and he nips at my throat.

I feel every inch of him inside me, and I want nothing more than to relish this feeling. I know that this moment is fleeting, but I want it to stay with me. I'm falling into oblivion. I'm not sure what I'm falling into, but I know this is peaceful. This is how I want to forever feel in this world. Nothing can touch me. Nothing can hurt me. Nothing can make me feel this good.

My lips touch his, his body trembles against me, and I feel his soul in my soul. My legs begin to tremble, my toes curling as I scream out. I'm so close. So damn close.

"Oh Christ, *now*, *Hannah*—come now," he shouts and plunges deep, filling me with his hot essence.

Because he does command my body, it responds immediately, the walls of my channel clenching and squeezing around his cock in the most satisfying—emotionally and physically—orgasm of my life.

Armando slows his rocking and showers kisses on my cheeks, eyelids, across the bridge of my nose. "I love you, beautiful girl."

"I love you, too," I croak, fighting my way back from the other galaxy where I'd been shot by my pleasure. I wrap my legs around his back and pull his hips in even tighter. "So much."

Chapter Thirty-Two

Armando

The scent of dirt, metal and blood hits my nose the minute I'm let into the warehouse.

It's three in the goddamn morning. I had to leave Hannah in my bed for this, which nearly killed me. But the don called me himself and told me to get down here. And when the don calls, you come. No questions. No complaints.

He could've dragged it out and made Emilio sweat his judgment, but instead the don chose to mete out the punishment tonight.

There are two parts of me now. The dead part. And the part Hannah made feel. The dead part doesn't give a shit what goes down tonight. Not if they bury Emilio at the bottom of Lake Michigan with a pair of cement shoes. Not even if they make me pull the trigger.

But the other part—the Hannah part—*fuck*. I can't stomach it. Like it physically makes me ill to think of Emilio getting whacked. Gracie being widowed before she even gets married. Not having her big wedding.

I don't like it.

It's not that I forgive the guy. He hired a hit on me just to save his own ass after stealing my girl.

The thing is, Grace isn't my girl anymore. Right now it feels like she never was. We were pretending. Going through the motions of what Made Men and their pretty, gold-digging girlfriends did.

I am in one of the don's warehouses in Little Italy, not far from Garden of Eden.

Emilio's curled up in the fetal position, bleeding and crying like a baby. The guys have already worked him over pretty good.

Everyone important is here. All the old-timers. Alex, Don G's son-in-law. Marco and Leo.

Don Pachino glances my way and lifts his chin to summon me. I walk over like the scene means nothing to me.

Which is only half true.

I've seen enough violence to harden me to the sight of it. Hell, I perpetrated enough violence to make Emilio think I was going to kill him when I got out. So the sight of him bruised and bleeding does nothing to me.

But knowing he might die soon? That makes me itchy.

"Emilio violated his oath." The room goes quiet when Don G speaks. This is it: Emilio's sentencing.

Looking around, I can tell I'm not the only guy who isn't entirely comfortable. Everyone looks grim. Hands stuffed in pockets, no hint of pleasure in any of it. Emilio may have fucked me, but he's still one of our own. He's Family. A brother-in-arms.

And he's been a favorite of the don's.

"He betrayed us all when he attempted to kill a member of La Famiglia."

Emilio lets out a sob, but he doesn't beg. He knows better.

Don G crosses his arms over his chest and lets his words settle over all of us. Lets the tension grow. "Armando, you are the injured party. What justice do you seek?"

Fuck.

I hoped the decision would be made for me.

"I'm not the only injured party," I say, looking toward Marco. "He got shot in the ass."

"And he's a bloody mess because of it," Marco says. "Don't worry. I got mine."

"You sure?" I ask. "You want to shoot him in the ass too. Seems only fair."

"I considered it," Marco says with a smirk.

Emilio peers up at me through the swollen slits his eyes have become. There's pleading in his gaze. Apology. "I'm sorry, Mando. I tried to cancel it, I swear to Christ, I did."

Of course, that reminds me of Hannah, which makes me feel again.

"Yeah, I know."

The room is silent. I don't think anyone even breathes.

"Hannah heard you calling it off."

I watch hope bloom on Emilio's face. He drags himself up on his forearms, then sits up with a wince, holding his ribs, which are undoubtedly broken.

I shove my hands in my pockets like the other men. Consider Emilio, the sorry *stronzo* at my feet. "You're such a fucking pansy, you couldn't even try to kill me yourself."

Tears fall down Emilio's face. He spreads his hands. "I'm sorry, Mando. I just love her so much. I always loved her. Even before you went in the can. I just wanted to live to marry her."

"How's that working out for you?"

I sense the agitation in the room at my dry threat. The implication that he wouldn't live to marry Grace.

I meet his pleading gaze. "Offer me restitution," I demand, throwing it out like a challenge. Like I might not accept his offer.

Relief and eagerness spread across his face. "Anything. I'll pay it. Name your price."

"How much is that wedding worth to you?"

"Anything," Emilio begs.

"Fifty thousand." I throw out the first number that pops in my head.

"One hundred," Don G interjects firmly.

Emilio nods eagerly, dragging himself slowly to his knees. "I'll pay it. Yes, of course. I'll pay it."

"Bring it to him tomorrow, and we'll put this to bed." He looks at me. "No retributions."

I hold my hands up. "I never threatened him in the first place. You told me to leave it, and I did." I lift my shoulders. "I follow orders. I'm loyal."

Unlike some other stronzo *fucks.* I don't say it, but I know everyone there's thinking the same thing.

Emilio will have to live with his shame for the rest of his life. He may still be in the Family, but he lost all respect tonight.

"Yes." Don G's glance slides back to Emilio with distaste. "I misjudged which direction the conflict would come from."

Fuck it. Hannah's love made me generous. Or maybe she's just working through me. That infinite abundance of non-judgment she seems to carry. I close the distance between me and Emilio and hold out my hand.

He looks at me doubtfully, like he still expects me to

pull out a gun and shoot him through the teeth, but I wait with my palm extended, steady.

When he finally takes it, I haul him to his feet. "Dumber things have been done to keep a woman. You be good to Grace." I pull him in for a bro-hug, and he grips my shoulder tightly, like I'm the only thing keeping him alive. Which I guess is sort of true.

The tension in the room releases all at once, grunts of approval going around.

"Don't—don't tell her," he begs when I release him.

I shake my head, totally cool. "Never. Nobody here will." It's probably true, but I look around to be sure, making it a warning.

Everyone nods his agreement.

Don G. turns and walks away, like he's not going to dignify Emilio with any more of his attention. He stops at the door. "Settle it by tomorrow. Mando, tell me when it's done. And then I don't ever want to hear of this shit again."

"*Capito, Capito,*" Emilio says, but Don G gives him his back again.

Marco saunters to my side, eying Emilio with disdain. "Well, I'd be worried, too, if I took your girl. You are a fucking badass."

It's a joke, and it lightens some of the tension in the room. Guys start moving around, talking to each other.

"My girl's waiting for me at home, so no offense, but I got better places to be."

"Go. Go home." Lorenzo makes a shooing motion. "Take care of that pregnant girl of yours."

Some of the guys grunt in surprise to hear my news.

I suspect Lorenzo's invested in me and Hannah and the baby since I entrusted him with their lives earlier. I might think about making him godfather. Although Marco would be a wiser choice, not just because he's younger.

That guy would saw off his own hand for me.

I clasp his hand, and we smack each other's shoulders.

"See you tomorrow, Emilio," I say without any taunt in my voice. I don't know how the guy is going to come up with a hundred grand by tomorrow, but it's not my problem.

Even if I offered to give him some time to pull it together, Don G would never stand for it.

He made his ruling. His will be done.

* * *

Hannah

Armando comes in at six in the morning.

I remember him getting a phone call and leaving. It must have been around three.

I sit up in bed, scared. Searching his face for bruises or blood, but apart from looking tired, he seems whole.

"Is everything okay?"

I don't ask where he's been. I know he can't tell me.

He nods. "It's good. Shit got resolved with Emilio."

Emilio. It's not like me to hold a grudge, but he put a hit on Armando, so I'm not sure I'll ever forgive him for that.

Still, I don't really want to hear he's dead, either. Not that Armando would share that with me if he was.

"Will there... still be a wedding for him and Grace?"

Armando shucks his clothing and comes to the bed. "Yeah. He's paying me restitution. Do you know what that means, Flowers?" He crawls toward me and pushes me back down, covering my body with his own.

I have absolutely no clue. "No?"

"It means I have money to invest in Garden of Eden. Our family business."

My eyes fill with tears.

Family business.

I don't think I realized how alone I've felt running Garden of Eden until this moment. I brought Josie on to try to lessen that burden, but she wasn't invested in it like I am.

But now I have Armando. And I already know this man can do anything. Which means, the business is saved. I know he'll help me straighten it out. Fix everything.

That's the kind of guy he is.

"That's it, baby. Cry me those tears. Are they happy ones?"

"Yes." I nod. "I'm happy."

He grins. It's a rare occurrence to see a smile on him, and it takes my breath away. "What are you happy about?"

"That we're a family."

His smile grows wider.

"You're my family, Flowers. You and that baby are everything to me."

I reach for him and pull him down.

After a searing kiss, he lifts his head. "You're mine, Hannah," he says, his voice low and possessive. "You're mine, and I'll do everything in my power to make you happy."

A shiver runs down my spine at the conviction in his words, but I don't shy away from them. Instead, I welcome them, wrapping my arms around his neck and pressing my lips to his. We kiss deeply, passionately, the world around us fading away as we lose ourselves in each other.

There's something about him that makes me feel safe, secure, like nothing can touch me as long as he's by my side.

I moan softly into his mouth as he nudges my legs apart.

He kisses every inch of my skin, starting with my neck and moving down my shoulders then to my breasts. I arch my back as his lips close around my nipple, his fingers slipping between my legs. I gasp as he enters me, his movements slow and deliberate.

But I want more than his fingers. I want his dick buried deep inside me. "More," I moan. "More."

I don't even realize what I'm doing until I'm on top of him after shedding him of his pants, my legs straddling his hips. I position myself, his dick pressing against my sex. The thick tip of his cock slips into me, and I gasp, my body momentarily stilling.

He's so fucking big, and this angle almost hurts.

But I like the pain. I love it.

I start to move, sliding up his length, the feeling of his thickness stretching me so much more intense than his fingers.

I'm impaling myself on his cock, my moans loud and throaty. His hands grip my hips, forcing me to ride his cock, his hips rising to meet mine, driving his cock deep inside me.

I throw my head back, throwing my hair behind me as I let myself go, my orgasm exploding through my body like fireworks in the night sky.

I ride him harder and faster, my body desperate for more, needing more. My nails dig into his shoulders, my hips bucking wildly against him. I'm moaning louder and louder, my cries of pleasure echoing through the room.

I slow to a stop, straddling him and staring him in the eye as I move myself up and down his cock. He looks at me like I'm the most beautiful woman in the world as I ride him, my movements slow and rhythmic.

My eyes flutter closed as I near my next orgasm.

"That's right," he whispers, his words soft and full of need. "Come for me, Hannah. Come for me."

His words push me into my orgasm, his words and his cock. I throw my head back and scream his name, my body quivering as I come again.

He flips me over on the bed and positions himself behind me, his cock sliding into me once more. His hands grip my hips, and he thrusts deep into me.

His cock pulses inside me, his body growing tense and tight. He thrusts a few more times before growing still. He moans deeply as his cock twitches inside me, his hot seed filling me.

He pulls out and lies beside me on the bed, pulling me against his body.

"I love you, Flowers."

I tuck my face against his neck, basking in the power of his words. In his love. His attention. His promise.

"I love you so much," I tell him.

"You brought me back from the dead. You gave me a reason to live. I owe you everything. I want you to know, I will never let you down again."

Tears spear my eyes once more. "I know you won't," I whisper against his skin.

I trust this man with my life. With our child. With our future.

He's my everything.

Epilogue

Hannah

"The judges have viewed all the entries and picked four finalists to compete. Will the following florists step forward..."

Armando's arm tightens around my thickened waist from behind. "It's gonna be you," he murmurs in my ear.

Marco and Leo both thump me on the back. I'm touched they came along. It's really true that Armando's family looks after one another. And that now includes me.

My heart taps a staccato beat against my ribs, but the truth is—I don't care if I don't make it to the finals. What's more important to me is this feeling in my chest now.

The pouring flow of love, of support from him. The pleasure of having the person I care about most in this world at my side for the moments that matter.

As he promised, Armando used Emilio's restitution payment to invest in Garden of Eden. He bought a new van and hired two part-time guys to make my deliveries. He's thrown himself into building the business—our *family business,* he calls it—and in the last two months, revenue has already tripled. He talked the don into making physical upgrades and is looking into a second location. All the stuff that used to terrify me, he's taken over, and he makes it look so easy. I can focus on what I'm good at—the artistic side, and we do the networking together, so it's less intimidating.

"Hannah Munn," the announcer says, and I gasp. I really didn't expect to make it to the finals.

"Told you," Armando rumbles in my ear before releasing me to go up on stage.

I draw in a shaky breath, shake out my hands and bend over to pick up my bucket of flowers.

"Stop," Armando scoffs. "I'll carry them up there."

He doesn't let me pick up anything heavy. Or stay on my feet for too long. Or work too hard. He treats me like a princess, except for in his bed. There, he still turns animal on me, even with my growing baby bump.

I make my way up there, and he follows, carrying my bucket full of flowers and setting it beside me on the floor. "Knock 'em dead, Flowers," he murmurs and squeezes my hand before he slips away, leaving me with the other contestants. The next step is to design an arrangement for them with flowers we provide while everyone watches. Then to make one with flowers they provide.

I wait for the timer then put together my arrangement. It's an artistic spiral of multi-colored roses interwoven with freesia and silver wicker wisps. When I finish and step back for the judges to view, I don't let myself look at the other three contestants' arrangements—I'm too nervous and doubt wants to creep in, hard. Instead, I find Armando in the audience. We lock gazes, and immediately, I sense his strength. His confidence in me. It pours into me, washing away the nerves. I attempt a small smile, and he grins back.

Full-on grin. Nothing makes me happier than seeing his

face crack a smile like that. Knowing I'm the one who helped revive him.

Last week was Grace and Emilio's wedding. I did my very best on the flowers—not because Emilio deserved it but because it's Armando's family, and I'm a part of it now. We attended the wedding as guests, as well. It was Armando's decision. He said he was too happy with me to hold a grudge with either of them.

The organizers bring us their buckets of flowers, and the next round begins. I don't think, just let my fingers pluck the flowers and arrange them, no plan in mind. I know if I start trying to figure out the right thing, I'll get it wrong. My creative genius happens when I don't edit, don't worry, don't think.

So I ride the bliss of Armando's love. The pleasure of wearing his ring and building a life, family and business with him. And the arrangement creates itself—a simple but striking multi-tiered arrangement of peonies and star-gazer lilies.

The timer dings. We step back. I catch Armando's eye, and he winks. Hope starts to leak in. I made it this far, it sure would be amazing to win. But no, I shouldn't let myself go there because what if I'm disappointed?

The judges confer, and I get a little dizzy waiting. The pregnancy's doing a number on my blood volume, or so my mom has told me. She's overjoyed with my pregnancy now that I'm happy. I think my dad is even starting to accept Armando although he doesn't like the fact that he's part of the mafia.

Armando says that's something he can't change, but he promises to shield me and our family from any of its negative effects. I know there are no guarantees. He could end up in prison again. Or be killed. But for the moment, the don is letting him stay out of the business to run mine. And it's hard not to feel invincible with his love wrapped so tightly around me.

"The judges have made their decision. In third place, Jaya Lowe." The crowd claps. I pretend I'm breathing. "In second place, Eric Diamond."

Crap. That probably means I didn't get it.

"In first place, the winner of this year's competition is... Hannah Munn, of Garden of Eden."

I hear Armando shout. I try to stop the waterworks already spewing from my eyes, but it's impossible. There will be no elegance and poise for me as I accept the trophy. But it doesn't matter.

I won.

I carry the trophy back to Armando on shaking legs, and he sweeps me off my feet into a spin. "You did it! I knew you would, Flowers."

"I can't stop crying." I say the obvious.

He sets me gently on my feet and kisses away the tears. "Keep crying, Flowers. It only gets better from here."

Also by Alta Hensley

<u>Gods Among Men Series:</u>

Villains Are Made

Monsters Are Hidden

Vipers Are Forbidden

* * *

<u>Secret Bride Trilogy:</u>

Captive Bride

Kept Bride

Taken Bride

* * *

<u>Wonderland Trilogy:</u>

King of Spades

Queen of Hearts

Ace of Diamonds

* * *

<u>Dark Pen Series:</u>

Devil's Contract

Dirty Ledger

Dangerous Notes

* * *

<u>Spiked Roses Billionaires' Club:</u>

Bastards & Whiskey

Villains & Vodka

Scoundrels & Scotch

Devils & Rye

Beasts & Bourbon

Sinners & Gin

* * *

<u>Evil Lies Series:</u>

The Truth About Cinder

The Truth About Alice

* * *

<u>Breaking Belles Series:</u>

Elegant Sins

Beautiful Lies

Opulent Obsession

Inherited Malice

Delicate Revenge

Lavish Corruption

* * *

Gold In Locks

Sick Crush

Secret Bride

Captive Vow

Ruin Me

Delicate Scars

Other Titles by Renee Rose

Chicago Sin

Den of Sins

Rooted in Sin

Made Men Series

Don't Tease Me

Don't Tempt Me

Don't Make Me

Chicago Bratva

"Prelude" in Black Light: Roulette War

The Director

The Fixer

"Owned" in Black Light: Roulette Rematch

The Enforcer

The Soldier

The Hacker

The Bookie

The Cleaner

The Player

The Gatekeeper

Alpha Mountain

Hero

Rebel

Warrior

Vegas Underground Mafia Romance

King of Diamonds

Mafia Daddy

Jack of Spades

Ace of Hearts

Joker's Wild

His Queen of Clubs

Dead Man's Hand

Wild Card

Contemporary
Daddy Rules Series

Fire Daddy

Hollywood Daddy

Stepbrother Daddy

Master Me Series

Her Royal Master

Her Russian Master

Her Marine Master

Yes, Doctor

Double Doms Series

Theirs to Punish

Theirs to Protect

Holiday Feel-Good

Scoring with Santa

Saved

Other Contemporary

Black Light: Valentine Roulette

Black Light: Roulette Redux

Black Light: Celebrity Roulette

Black Light: Roulette War

Black Light: Roulette Rematch

Punishing Portia (written as Darling Adams)

The Professor's Girl

Safe in his Arms

Paranormal

Two Marks Series

Untamed

Tempted

Desired

Enticed

Wolf Ranch Series

Rough

Wild

Feral

Savage

Fierce

Ruthless

Wolf Ridge High Series

Alpha Bully

Alpha Knight

Step Alpha

Bad Boy Alphas Series

Alpha's Temptation

Alpha's Danger

Alpha's Prize

Alpha's Challenge

Alpha's Obsession

Alpha's Desire

Alpha's War

Alpha's Mission

Alpha's Bane

Alpha's Secret

Alpha's Prey

Alpha's Sun

Shifter Ops

Alpha's Moon

Alpha's Vow

Alpha's Revenge
Alpha's Fire
Alpha's Rescue
Alpha's Command

Midnight Doms

Alpha's Blood
His Captive Mortal
All Souls Night

Alpha Doms Series

The Alpha's Hunger
The Alpha's Promise
The Alpha's Punishment
The Alpha's Protection (Dirty Daddies)

Other Paranormal

The Winter Storm: An Ever After Chronicle

Sci-Fi

Zandian Masters Series

His Human Slave
His Human Prisoner
Training His Human
His Human Rebel
His Human Vessel
His Mate and Master

Zandian Pet

Their Zandian Mate

His Human Possession

Zandian Brides

Night of the Zandians

Bought by the Zandians

Mastered by the Zandians

Zandian Lights

Kept by the Zandian

Claimed by the Zandian

Stolen by the Zandian

Other Sci-Fi

The Hand of Vengeance

Her Alien Masters

About Alta Hensley

Alta Hensley is a USA TODAY bestselling author of hot, dark and dirty romance. She is also an Amazon Top 10 bestselling author. Being a multi-published author in the romance genre, Alta is known for her dark, gritty alpha heroes, sometimes sweet love stories, hot eroticism, and engaging tales of the constant struggle between dominance and submission.

She lives in a log cabin in the woods with her husband, two daughters, and an Australian Shepherd. When she isn't battling the bats, and watching the deer, she is writing about villains who always get their love story and happily ever after.

Facebook: https://www.facebook.com/AltaHensleyAuthor/
Amazon: https://www.amazon.com/Alta-Hensley/e/B004G5A6LI
Website: www.altahensley.com
Instagram: https://instagram.com/altahensley
Bookbub: https://www.bookbub.com/authors/alta-hensley
TikTok: https://www.tiktok.com/@altahensley
Join her mailing list: https://landing.mailerlite.com/webforms/landing/c9b6n3

About Renee Rose

USA TODAY BESTSELLING AUTHOR RENEE ROSE loves a dominant, dirty-talking alpha hero! She's sold over two million copies of steamy romance with varying levels of kink. Her books have been featured in USA Today's *Happily Ever After* and *Popsugar*. Named Eroticon USA's Next Top Erotic Author in 2013, she has also won *Spunky and Sassy's* Favorite Sci-Fi and Anthology author, *The Romance Reviews* Best Historical Romance, and *has* hit the *USA Today* list over a dozen times with her Chicago Bratva, Bad Boy Alpha and Wolf Ranch series, as well as various anthologies.

Renee loves to connect with readers!
www.reneeroseromance.com
renee@reneeroseromance.com

- facebook.com/reneeroseromance
- twitter.com/reneeroseauthor
- instagram.com/reneeroseromance
- amazon.com/Renee-Rose/e/B008AS0FT0
- bookbub.com/authors/renee-rose
- tiktok.com/@authorreneerose

www.ingramcontent.com/pod-product-compliance
Lightning Source LLC
LaVergne TN
LVHW011815060526
838200LV00053B/3790